FOR LOVE OF FAMILY

A NOVEL BY
C. R. Boonstra

FOR LOVE OF
FAMILY

TATE PUBLISHING & *Enterprises*

For Love of Family
Copyright © 2011 by C.R. Boonstra. All rights reserved.

No part of this publication may be reproduced, stored in a retrieval system or transmitted in any way by any means, electronic, mechanical, photocopy, recording or otherwise without the prior permission of the author except as provided by USA copyright law.

This novel is a work of fiction. Names, descriptions, entities, and incidents included in the story are products of the author's imagination. Any resemblance to actual persons, events, and entities is entirely coincidental. However, several names, descriptions, entities, and incidents included in the story are based on the lives of real people.

This book is designed to provide accurate and authoritative information with regard to the subject matter covered. This information is given with the understanding that neither the author nor Tate Publishing, LLC is engaged in rendering legal, professional advice. Since the details of your situation are fact dependent, you should additionally seek the services of a competent professional.

The opinions expressed by the author are not necessarily those of Tate Publishing, LLC.

Published by Tate Publishing & Enterprises, LLC
127 E. Trade Center Terrace | Mustang, Oklahoma 73064 USA
1.888.361.9473 | www.tatepublishing.com

Tate Publishing is committed to excellence in the publishing industry. The company reflects the philosophy established by the founders, based on Psalm 68:11,
"The Lord gave the word and great was the company of those who published it."

Book design copyright © 2011 by Tate Publishing, LLC. All rights reserved.
Cover design by Amber Gulilat
Interior design by Joel Uber

Published in the United States of America
ISBN: 978-1-61739-699-1
1. Fiction; Romance, General
2. Fiction; General
11.01.24

DEDICATION

This book is first dedicated to my dear wife Peggy, then to our children and grandchildren, along with our parents. Each has a special place in my heart, as we share life together.

THE CAMPOUT

The quietness was overwhelming for thirty-two-year-old Beca Stone. Rustic camping was not her idea of a new experience, but somehow her girlfriends Rhonda and Jillian had talked her into a weekend of exploring. The taco she grabbed on the way to Rhonda's home didn't sit well, or maybe it was the nerves from a busy week at the store where she worked. When camp was set up her two friends went hiking, leaving the ailing Beca on the site alone with her thoughts.

Life was not turning out exactly the way she had imagined it might as a young girl. She envied her friends by desiring a family like they had. Having her own house in the country with a few flower gardens and spending time with friends and family was nice, but Beca still felt some emptiness, although she would never actually admit it to her friends.

Her parents, Josh and Elaine, seemed to have a wonderful marriage and the perfect family with Beca and her younger brother, Jake. Growing up she felt loved and cared for, even admiring her predictable father, who had driven truck for the same meat company the last thirty-four years.

All three friends had looked forward to this weekend with the campfires, hiking, telling jokes, and catching up on lives. This had been a busy week at the store where she worked, and the camping trip with friends was a good way to unwind, reflect on life, and throw caution to the wind.

The quiet began fading away as Beca heard the voices of her two friends approaching the campsite. Jillian was rather excited as she blurted out, "You won't believe what we saw."

Of course that immediately got Beca's attention, so she questioned, "What! What was it?"

Both girls in harmony shouted, "A raccoon with babies!"

Then Jillian remarked, "I think we scared them as much as they scared us, and we ran halfway back here before we ran out of breath."

By this time Beca was feeling better and was ready to join in the activities. First they needed to gather firewood before the darkness set in, so the three friends went in different directions with the challenge of who could drag the biggest piece of firewood back.

Soon they had accumulated a substantial pile of wood to keep the early evening chill at bay. It was June in Michigan, but the nights were still cool. At least it wasn't suppose to rain for a few days.

Darkness was setting in as the friends settled into the chairs around the fire. Rhonda made the comment that this was the first time since she and her husband had started camping that it was girls only. She was excited to be spending this special time with her two best friends.

After what seemed like only minutes due to the non-stop chatting, they realized it actually had been a couple hours. The fire had died down, and the warm sleeping bag had become very inviting.

Startled, Beca sat up quickly. What was that noise and how could it be light out already? She thought being in the great outdoors must have really made her tired, because she had slept better than being in her own bed.

Crawling out of the tent, she found herself the last one up, with her friends cutting her no slack by asking if she got her beauty sleep.

Looking around, she realized the noise was just a few squirrels scampering through nearby trees. She wondered how something so small could make such a racket. "They are kinda cute as long as they stay beyond the campsite," she mumbled under her breath.

Waking up quickly when the smell of the pancakes Jillian was cooking on the camp stove reached her nose, she approached the others and blurted out, "I'm so hungry it really doesn't matter what's on the menu."

Jillian quickly commented that a few bugs got mixed up in the pancake batter, a smile slowly crossing her face.

How could anyone ask for better friends? The three had shared their lives since childhood, all living in the same neighborhood just a few houses apart. Rhonda was a year older, married Roger at nineteen, and had a son Graham after a couple of years, with her daughter Christine, following only thirteen months later.

Rhonda was a stay-at-home mom who said she would do it all the same way if she had to do it again. She was always so full of life.

Jillian only four months younger than Beca, married Chad Mills a year after meeting him in college. They waited to have their only child, James, because she wanted time to use the education acquired for teaching elementary school.

When James was born five years ago, Jillian took two years off to spend the precious, valuable time with her son. Now she was back teaching fourth graders. The kids seemed to love her as much as she looked forward to seeing them each day.

"Lost in your thoughts?"

The voice behind Beca startled her, almost causing her to dump what was left of her breakfast on the ground.

Rhonda laughed at the sight of her friend's confusion, before sympathetically apologizing for sneaking up on her.

Rhonda had packed a lunch for the three of them and already had it in her backpack. There was no discussion as to what Beca had to do, other than get her hiking shoes on.

Personally, she hoped the hike wouldn't be very long. She really wanted some relax time just to sit by the campfire with a book and maybe even a hot cup of coffee. However, she also knew she could do that anytime, due to the status of living alone with her cat, Missy.

This was the kind of entertainment her friends wanted and needed as an outlet to life's stresses. Although she felt fairly fit, she knew the exercise wouldn't hurt her any either. She actually looked forward to the bonding time as they started up the trail for their day of adventure.

The first couple of hours flew by as they concentrated on the trail, and all the interesting things of nature that the woods around them displayed. A slight breeze made this the perfect temperature for the activities of the day, with the scenery around them eventually changing from ridges, gullies and trees, to a flat open area.

In time they decided to rest the feet and feed the stomach. So, out came the snacks; they sat for a few minutes on a couple of large rocks, while reviewing the guide map. Rhonda checked the GPS she had brought along, stating they were over eight miles from the campsite as the crow flies.

Beca soon began to understand, just how long the hike was really going to be when Rhonda and Jillian talked of how they both wanted to take the long way back to camp. Hoping to linger in the present place a little longer, she intentionally started a conversation by saying, "I don't look forward to another lonely summer."

The response was just what she had hoped for as Jillian abruptly turned toward her with a bewildered look and inquired, "What do you mean?"

"Well, you know. I have nobody to share my life with like you guys do."

Rhonda who was anxious to keep hiking, sarcastically asked, "Did we come to talk or hike?"

Ignoring the comment, Beca continued speaking to Jillian, "Sometimes I get jealous, especially when you talk of all the exciting things you do as a family. You probably even think my life is easy, not having anybody to answer to or be responsible for, but lately life seems routine—even boring. I know I'm not a spring chicken anymore, so if something is going to happen in my love life, it had better be soon!"

Rhonda, now feeling guilty for blowing off the initial comment, mustered up a quick apology before stating, "It's never too late, especially when you have two caring friends like us to help."

"Yeah, that's right," Jillian injected. "I'm sure if we put our heads together we can find someone for you." She hesitated briefly before saying in a questionable manner, "If that's what you want."

Silence fell as the two girls patiently waited for their friends reply, but none came.

Sensing the awkwardness, Rhonda leaned over, picked up her backpack, and boldly started up the trail, saying in an assertive voice, "Daylight is burning."

The other two got the message and quickly followed.

The noon sun was starting to give its heat as the three decided the ridge they were on offered a great view for eating lunch. While getting the food out of the backpack, they noticed two people coming up the trail in the direction they were headed.

"So much for isolation," commented Rhonda, who seemed to relish the fact they had seen nobody all morning.

Beca found comfort knowing there were other people in such a desolate area, but said nothing. It was a couple, and they approached at a quicker pace than the three girls had been keeping. When they reached the trio, it became apparent they also enjoyed seeing other people. They stopped to chat for a few minutes, excitedly telling how they had seen six deer approximately a mile back. After drinking from their water bottles and spending a few more minutes talking, the couple wished them safe hiking and proceeded down the ridge the girls had just come up.

"This is so exciting!" exclaimed Jillian as she finished her egg salad sandwich and spanned the wonderful sights of nature they could take in from their position on the ridge. "I'm so glad we decided to do this." She hesitated as if deep in thought, then added, "Looks like the weather is even cooperating."

"Two minutes to finish," stated Rhonda. "We want to make it back in time for the fire-roasted chicken I had planned for tonight's dinner."

With that incentive, the other two were on their feet saying "let's go."

Talking had subsided as the afternoon heat and the morning hike were taking a toll on their energy level. The girls listened to the woods around them and even hoped to see the deer the couple had mentioned.

Beca had gone hiking with her friends before but not for such a long trek. At least now they were headed back toward the campsite, giving her new enthusiasm. She was so looking forward to relaxing in that camping chair.

"Over there," whispered Jillian as she pointed through the trees at four deer in the distance.

The girls thought they were far enough away not to spook them, but remained as quiet and still as possible for a few moments.

The next half hour was uneventful, until, "Oh, no!" exclaimed Rhonda, who was leading. "I think we have a problem." She simply pointed to the trail ahead, indicating her reason for concern.

It seemed water had flooded the path for a short distance. Jillian spoke what the others were thinking, "How did the other hikers get past this? Why didn't they warn us about it? Well, I guess our options are get wet or find a way around it."

Beca mentioned they had no idea how deep it might be or the fact they could trip over something really creepy, making her friends laugh.

"Well, I guess we find a way around it," stated Rhonda, who immediately started for higher ground.

The trek led them over a few logs and up a steep, sandy slope. It took extra effort, but it paid off as they were soon back on the trail, past the water obstruction and with dry feet.

"I am hitting the sack early tonight!" exclaimed Beca. "I think this is the most exercise I've gotten in one day since I moved from the apartment into my house."

Jillian chimed in, "I think we will all sleep well, and I even suggest we sleep in tomorrow." She briefly glanced at Rhonda to see what reaction might be expressed. "Whatever the activities are, they can wait for a couple of hours. We came to relax and have fun, not abuse ourselves and go home tired."

Rhonda knew her friends well; that's why she pushed them to hike the first day out. Now she had her hiking fix and was willing to stay by the campsite the rest of the weekend. She stopped to check her GPS before stating they had walked almost twenty-two miles so far, and theoretically the campsite was about a half mile ahead.

The hike had been fun but the day long. When they arrived back at the site, Jillian volunteered to start the fire. Rhonda got out the chicken for the evening meal as Beca removed her shoes and massaged her sore feet, before slipping on a pair of comfortable sandals. As all three joined in to prepare the meal, it started to cloud over, and the wind began picking up, Jillian looked skyward and boldly exclaimed, "It better not rain! I ordered clear and dry!"

Fire-roasted chicken with baked beans right out of the can was definitely a camping experience to be remembered. The weekend was all about making memories with friends, and food always played a major part in any weekend campout. In the early evening, the wind died down as the sun began to set, causing it to feel much cooler. The girls brought out sweatshirts and sat by the campfire as darkness slowly crept in.

Jillian had not forgotten the conversation Beca had initiated during their hike, and curiosity won out over consideration. Trying to be subtle in her approach, she slyly pulled Rhonda in by asking an open-ended question to nobody in particular. "Who do we know that might be a good match for our friend? What kind of man is she looking for?"

Beca had been staring into the fire but quickly looked up at her friends, wondering if she should comment or let them suggest a few possibilities.

Jillian smiled mischievously then suggested, "How about one that drools, takes a bath once a week, and is missing half his teeth?"

Beca wrinkled her face in disapproval and said, "Be serious guys."

Soon all three of them summed up the criteria needed to be worthy: tall, dark, handsome, a good personality—gentle, energetic, spontaneous, smart, funny, and clean cut.

"Come on," Beca blurted out. "What are the odds someone like that is out there looking for me?"

Rhonda placed a flashlight under her chin lighting up just portions of her face, and in a monotone voice replied, "He is looking for you."

All three laughed spontaneously, and the conversation subsided as they continued sitting by the slowly dying fire. With the long day of vigorous exercise and the cool night air, the trio finally resorted to calling it a day.

Rhonda thought she had heard something during the night outside the tent, and now that morning was here, so was the evidence of raccoons having had a party of their own. Apparently the three friends had been so tired last night, some of the food was not put back in the car for security.

The animals must have appreciated the easy meal; garbage was strewn about the campsite. Rhonda cleaned up the site, gathered more firewood, started the fire, and had everything almost ready for a breakfast of eggs and toast with corned beef hash before Jillian and Beca even emerged from the tent.

As Beca slowly embraced the morning, she looked over at Rhonda and asked, "Do you ever slow down?"

Jillian commented, "Rhonda has always been the one to lead, push, challenge, and keep us on our toes. We know her philosophy has always been *it's the journey not the destination*. We hang around her just for the inspiration."

Just as the three friends were sitting down for breakfast, they heard a male voice call out to them. "Excuse me, ladies," the man politely stated as he approached them. "My friends and I came in late last night, only to discover this morning we forgot our matches. Is it possible to borrow a few from you so we can cook our breakfast? By the way I'm Sal, Sal Bingly."

Rhonda responded, "My name is Rhonda, and I don't see any reason we can't be hospitable to our neighbors." She got back up and retrieved a few matches from their stash. As she handed them to him, she spoke so softly that her friends couldn't make out what she said.

Thanking them, he left immediately.

"What did you say to him?" inquired Jillian.

"Nothing really," she lied. "I just told him not to let the fire go out or something like that."

Soon breakfast was done along with the cleanup, so they stocked the fire and took up residence around it. They had barely gotten comfortable, when once again they heard a male voice ask, "Do you have room for a few more around that fire?"

Looking up, Beca noted three men with chairs in hand, quickly approaching.

WEEKEND MOMMY

"Took you up on the offer to sit by the fire a few minutes," stated Sal.

Jillian and Beca both gave their friend a look of concern. They didn't know these guys and definitely hadn't discussed sharing their campfire. They could only surmise Rhonda had invited them when Sal borrowed the matches, but why?

Sal sensed the discomfort and apologized for their unexpected intrusion. He introduced his friends and indicated they would leave immediately if anybody felt uncomfortable. The bright morning sun majestically erased the tension, and the other two girls welcomed them.

Once seated, Sal introduced his friends Tim and Larry, explaining how their campout was supposed to be two nights, but sudden work schedules deterred them. Even so, he explained, "We still wanted to get out here, even if it was for one night." Then he made special effort to point out that Tim, the only single guy, was the reason for their shortened weekend.

Suddenly it dawned on Beca what Rhonda had done. Somehow in a manner only she could muster, she had told Sal to come back if one of the men with him was available; she was playing matchmaker with strangers. Nonchalantly, she turned her head to peer at her conniving friend. Rhonda was grinning from ear to ear as if to say, "So what do you think?"

Tim was handsome by most standards, but why was this mid-thirties man single? Then she scolded herself for the thought as she considered her own position in life.

The six adults shared the fire and conversation for almost an hour before the three men decided not to overstay their welcome and parted.

"So what do you think?" Rhonda asked, with the guys still almost within earshot. "That was underhanded, uncalled for, and potentially dangerous!" scolded Beca.

"I saw an opportunity and tried to help a friend," came the rebuttal.

"But you knew nothing about these guys, absolutely nothing! So how did you do it anyway?"

"Well, when I gave Sal the matches, I gave him a short message. I believe I said, 'if you have a single guy with you come back after breakfast to sit by the fire.' Rather short and to the point. I guess he picked up on it okay because they showed up.

"Well, nice try," Beca scowled. "He didn't ask for my phone number, so I guess we already know the outcome."

After that Rhonda only sat at the campfire sporadically. With her energy and lack of sit-ability, she was always off exploring something nearby. When Rhonda came back from her latest trek, Jillian informed her they needed to start thinking seriously about helping Beca find the man of her dreams. "Maybe this weekend had a purpose beyond our expectations. I was trying to do my part," Rhonda stated proudly.

Monday morning brought back the normal routine for Beca. She scarfed down a quick bowl of cereal after her morning shower; work was waiting, and she didn't like being late to the store. Why did she call it a store? Being a wholesale plumbing company didn't involve the contact a retail store did. Her particular job involved even less contact as she inventoried, invoiced, and kept the paperwork straight. She remembered the excitement when she was hired almost eight years ago, after working several dead-end and part-time jobs, the first few years after high school. Maybe she should have gone to college like Jillian had so she too could have met Mr. Right; maybe then her life would be drastically different than it was now.

The week flew by. Beca tried to catch up on the yard work she had neglected last week just because she just didn't feel like it; now it was payback time. She still had not planted all the flowers she had anticipated for the year, or trimmed the trees that so badly needed it, and now it was already well into June. It seemed this time of year the lawn needed mowing twice a week, monopolizing the evenings.

Between her job, the yard, and housework, she didn't seem to have any extra energy or time lately. She was thankful her father had taught her how to care for things around the house, even if it wasn't appreciated when growing up. Life really was good, except for the emptiness she felt by being alone. It seemed like everybody around had someone to share life with. She still held hope that someday she might have someone too.

Thursday evening, Rhonda called to chat for a few minutes. Beca suspected it was to check up on her like her friends did periodically in subtle ways. She appreciated it and never let on that she knew what they were up to. After some small talk, she made an excuse about her cat needing attention and told Rhonda good-bye.

Friday after work Beca received a call from Jillian, asking her if she'd be willing to take five-year-old James the next weekend like she had done a few times before. Jillian and Chad wanted to go to Chicago for a weekend getaway and needed a sitter. She loved little James, who called her "Auntie Beca." She loved the energy he brought into her life. She quickly checked her schedule before eagerly replying, "I'd be happy to."

She wondered how anybody could be so lucky, having friends that included her in their lives at every opportunity. They were always there to listen and help, without judging. They were her extended family, and she felt a special connection to their children.

The phone rang on Sunday evening. Picking it up, Beca was surprised when Tim, the mid-thirties man from the campground, introduced himself. Although surprised, she was intrigued and asked how he had gotten her number, especially since she had never even given him her full name.

He cautiously chose his words when he mentioned how her friend Rhonda had visited his campsite later that same day, giving the information to him. "That figures!" she blurted out before quickly apologizing for shouting in his ear. "She has a mind of her own, and I know she means well, so I'll let it slip for now."

"I called to see if I could take you out to dinner," he quickly injected before she could start blabbering again. "I'd like to spend an evening alone with you instead of having a group analysis."

She was smitten by his humor and consented to going out. She suddenly remembered her commitment to watch James for the weekend, then felt a twinge of guilt for wishing she had the weekend open.

She explained her previous commitment for the upcoming weekend to him. He was silent for only a few seconds before responding, "What about next week, Tuesday evening? That gives you an evening between to recuperate, and a weeknight works for me."

She really was curious who Tim was and didn't want to keep pushing him away for fear he might get the wrong message, so she agreed to be picked up at six for dinner the following Tuesday evening. She then gave him the directions to her home. Placing the phone back in its cradle, she whispered to Missy, "I have a date."

The next week dragged by as Beca anticipated little James coming for the weekend. She was so looking forward to it, making mental plans for going out to eat thinking, *well at least I have someone to go with*. She hardly ever went out alone to a sit-down restaurant, it just seemed a bit awkward. Maybe he could help her plant some flowers in the yard, or maybe they could throw a ball, even take a walk to the park down the street. She knew little James loved the park.

Beca had one other love in life, and that was her hobby of bicycling. It was her way of relaxing, keeping in shape, and getting out in the wonderful world of ever-changing scenery. She had always liked biking with her dad and brother Jake, when she was young.

For a high school graduation present, her parents had purchased for her an eighteen-speed mountain bike. Somehow it had seemed impractical at the time, she thought it easier to drive, and she already had a bike if she wanted to take an occasional ride. But her parents in their wisdom had made an investment in the future, apparently knowing her interest better than she did. She would probably have it for the rest of her life, and it was a top quality bike, she especially liked the comfortable gel seat.

When Jillian and Chad dropped James off on Friday, Beca had just gotten home from work. Chad was eager to get going due to the long drive they had ahead of them that night. Beca didn't have time to shower or prepare any food for the evening, but Jillian had thought of the situation ahead of time and had prepared a smoky link and bean casserole that James liked.

After they left and the meal was done, Beca thought that they should start having fun right away. So she asked James if he would like to go to the park for a little while, besides she reasoned, I haven't had my shower yet, so what's a little more dirt? Of course James was all for that idea, so they started for the park a few blocks down the road.

After about an hour, Beca told James it was time to head back to the house to which he complied without any issues, he had always listened well to his auntie. It didn't take long after cleaning up James and putting his superman pajamas on, before he was out. The activities at the park tired both of them out, so Beca took her shower then relaxed in her La-Z-Boy chair.

Having just dozed off, the ringing phone startled her. It was Jillian checking in to see if all was well with her son, James. Beca assured her it was, relaying how they had gone to the park, tiring both of them out.

Beca opened her eyes as she heard a soft voice asking, "Auntie Beca are you sleeping?"

There was James right up in her face, and she realized she would not be sleeping in this Saturday! James attempted to open her eyelid and asked, "Can we eat now? I hungry." So she told James to wait in the kitchen and she would be right out to get them breakfast.

Finally awake, Beca realized it was raining outside. *Great*, she thought, *there goes my day in the yard with James idea.* Now she would have to come up with a different game plan to keep James entertained. After breakfast she got out a few toys her friends had donated over the years for such occasions. While James played, she took care of the laundry and dishes.

"All right, James," stated Beca. "I think we are going shopping for a little while. Let's get you dressed."

James liked spending time with her, especially when they went shopping, because he usually ended up getting a new toy of some sort. This was not the day she had planned, but Beca did need to pick a few things up, so off they went. First to the dollar store just to see what good deal she could find on something she probably didn't really need, and to find James something special from his auntie, then to the grocery store for a few needed items.

When they returned home, it seemed the rain was letting up, but it was still too wet outside to do anything in the yard. So they played a game inside until it was time for lunch. After lunch Beca thought maybe they could venture outside, things were finally drying out. She was glad James was so well behaved, thinking maybe someday she would like to have a child of her own just like him.

James squealed with excitement as he ran around the yard releasing bottled up energy. Beca was enjoying the fresh smelling air the rain had left behind and decided now was a good time to trim a few trees. She told James they needed to take a walk to the garage. After grabbing the pruning clippers, Beca trimmed branches and James helped by pulling them into a pile nearby. It didn't take long to do the trimming; now she wondered why it had been put off for so long. A feeling of satisfaction came over her for a job well done as now one more project was completed.

With the weather now cooperating, and still a few hours left before the evening meal, Beca asked James if he would like to help her go pick out flowers to plant around the yard. James, with his big brown eyes looking up at her, replied softly, "Okay auntie, but can we have a snack first?"

The softness of his voice and the pleading in his eyes melted Beca. She replied softly, "Of course we can."

So, they ventured into the house to cleanup a bit, then grabbed a few cookies before climbing into the car and heading for the garden center.

Beca loved the smells and the yard decorations at the garden center. It was a positive place she enjoyed being at. She was glad when she had gotten her own home, taking care of it gave her something to do in the evenings, plus there was the added satisfaction of seeing things grow that she had a hand in.

It only took a few minutes to find black-eyed Susans and a flat of petunias, which was what Beca had mentally noted for placement in her yard this year. She knew the black-eyed Susan flowers came back each year, saving her effort and money next year. They would also make the yard colorful year after year, without much work. Although it was a short drive back to the house, James fell asleep in the car, but as soon as they stopped in the driveway, he abruptly woke and was eager to help plant the flowers.

Beca looked at James as they finished the last of the flowers and exclaimed, "How could so much dirt be stuck to such a little boy?"

James just laughed as he wiped his hands on his pants and said, "Sorry Auntie, I help plant flowers."

"Okay, James," she whispered softly, lets put the tools away and get you cleaned up. I think it's bath time, young man."

While James was in the bathtub, Beca made the decision they would stay home to eat instead of going out as she had originally planned. She grabbed chicken strips from the freezer and threw them on the grill for the two of them. She liked to grill if sharing the meal with someone, besides she knew James loved chicken, cottage cheese, and chocolate milk; it all just happened to be on tonight's menu. Beca liked to spoil James once in a while, and he deserved it tonight for helping her plant the flowers and for being as good as a five-year-old could be. After the evening meal, they watched television together until it was time for James to go to bed; he went willingly after such a full day.

Sunday dawned with a colorful sunrise, which brought a smile to Beca's face as she felt the warmth of the sun streaming into the house. James was already up and playing quietly in the living room with Missy as Beca emerged to greet the day.

Upon seeing Beca, James asked, "What are we doing today, Auntie?"

She replied, "We are going to church after we have our breakfast." Then she got out the cold cereal and milk for a quick, easy meal.

As they headed out to church, James asked what church they were going to. She informed him they were going to the Bible church, which she had attended since she was a small girl.

Beca's parents were involved in the church, however she didn't see the need to be there all the time but did enjoy the social connections, singing, and inspiring messages.

Growing up in the church, Beca had been friends with Lisa Lows. They were the same age but had attended different schools, so the only place they ever saw each other was at church. They vowed to always be friends as young girls, now they were grown and both still attended the same church but lived opposite directions from it. They rarely did anything together, but when they did, it was as if they were still young, sharing their most intimate thoughts, while fully trusting each other.

Beca had never taken James to church before, and could tell he was nervous, probably because he did not know what to expect. He shyly asked, "Auntie, are you going to leave me by myself at the church?"

She instantly had compassion as she smiled at James and stated, "No way. I want to show my little boy off to all my friends."

At that James seemed content and remained quiet until arriving at the church.

Beca got lost in her thoughts during the church service, thinking to herself, *someday I'll have a little boy just like James*, who ironically was being exceptionally well behaved. Beca wondered if maybe he was too scared in his new surroundings to cause any problems. Before she knew it the service was wrapping up, and she was feeling guilty for not really paying attention.

Her friends and acquaintances quickly surrounded her and James after the service because they just had to find out who the cute little guy was. It was no surprise as people were always asking if she was dating or seeing anybody. Most of them seemed genuinely concerned for her, thinking she was a nice girl who shouldn't be alone. Usually she just brushed them off, but today she actually had a man to show everybody and relished the attention James was bringing her.

During lunch Beca suggested to James they go to the park again for a little while, because they had a few hours before his parents would be picking him up. It was a mistake to mention it before they had finished eating. James got all excited and could hardly sit long enough to finish. It seemed he had done all his sitting that morning in church, now it was time for some activity.

They couldn't have asked for better weather, almost eighty degrees with a light breeze blowing through the trees. Beca sat on a park bench and let James play on all the different playground equipment. She could keep a close eye on him as she relaxed on the bench, but that didn't last long. "Auntie Beca," James inquired. "Can you push me on the swing?"

These were precious memories they were making, and it seemed the rest of the world was miles away. Beca momentarily felt like she was a child once again, playing in the park. The time flew quickly by, and she soon realized they needed to get back, because she didn't know exactly when Jillian and Chad would show up to take her bundle of energy away from her. There were no regrets having James for the weekend, but she did begin to wonder if she could keep up with him all the time like Jillian did. They had not been back to the house more than ten minutes when James squealed, "Mommy, Daddy," as Chad and Jillian pulled into the driveway.

Jillian was walking toward the door, and James was running out to meet her. She quickly grabbed him in a big hug, asking multiple questions. "How is Mommy's big boy? Were you good for your auntie Beca? Did you have fun? What did you do?"

James was overwhelmed with all the questions and just hugged his mom tightly. Jillian finally was able to put James down, looking at Beca as she commented, "I know we're back sooner than you probably expected, but Chad wanted to catch some of the game today."

The girls exchanged light talk about what took place over the weekend, while Chad and James gathered all the items they needed to take back home with them. Then they patiently waited for the girls to finish.

After the Mills family had left, the house seemed extremely quiet to Beca. On one hand, she relished the peace, and on the other, envied her friends for always having someone around to share their lives with. The first few years out of school there had been a few dates, but it just didn't seem to click the way she thought it should. Maybe the expectations were high, but Beca took commitments seriously. She just knew there had to be someone special for her, so she continued to wait patiently for him to find her.

Her thoughts drifted back to Travis Webb from high school. He was a year or so older than her and had even shown some interest, but in her ignorance she always seemed to have other priorities. Now for the life of her she couldn't remember what could have been so important. She secretly admired him, but maybe she should not have hidden her adoration. Travis moved in not too far from her neighborhood when he was in the ninth grade, but suddenly moved out late in his junior year of high school, never returning. She never knew what happened to him.

She jumped as the ringing phone startled her, quickly bringing her back to the present. It was her mom asking how the weekend went with little James. Beca was happy to report it had been a fast, but happy time with him as she gave only vague information. Then her mom asked, "Did you remember dad and I are taking a trip to Branson, Missouri, for the next week? Could you please check on the house a few times?"

"Of course," Beca answered, but she thought to herself, *my life is a fill in the gap for everybody else's life.* At least she felt needed for something.

"Well, Beca," she stated out loud to her empty house, "it's time to pamper yourself." She started running warm water for a relaxing bath, then lit a couple candles before slipping a favorite CD in the player that she kept in the bathroom. After the relaxing bath, she made herself a bowl of popcorn, then plopped in front of the television. Sitting there she suddenly realized, just how worn out she really was from the last couple of days with James.

Her cat Missy must have been feeling neglected too. She jumped into Beca's lap and spilled some of the freshly made popcorn. "Missy!" shouted Beca angrily, to which the cat freaked out and jumped away quickly, spilling the rest of the popcorn. Beca spent the next few minutes cleaning up the mess before making more popcorn, because she really wanted some tonight. Before she sat back down, Beca found the cat and gave her some attention, just to make sure there would be no repeat of what had just happened.

It can't be morning already, thought Beca as she blinked due to the bright sun shining in her bedroom. "Oh, no!" she exclaimed when glancing at the clock. Suddenly realizing it was Monday, and she had forgotten to set the alarm last night. Now she would be late for work. Being late for anything was not her style, and she knew the harassment her coworkers would unleash on her. Not wasting any time, she quickly got dressed, skipped breakfast, and started immediately for work.

Only fifteen minutes late was still enough to be given a "what for" from her coworkers. Thankfully things settled down quickly, and Beca buried herself in her work. Having skipped breakfast, her stomach was growling, so she decided to take an early lunch.

The local grocery store had a deli, and today she had a taste for a sub sandwich, so she headed toward the store only about a mile from the plumbing store she worked at. Waiting to turn into the store parking lot, she was suddenly jolted forward as she heard a crunch.

Someone had just run into the back of her car. *I think I'm okay*, she thought to herself, but she soon realized her car was not when she tried but couldn't open her door; it had been jammed with the impact. *Great*, she thought. *I just got my Regal paid for*. She had bought the two-year-old car just three years ago and had worked hard to pay it off early.

THE ENCOUNTER

The rap on her window jarred Beca back to reality. "Are you all right?" A thirty something aged man was asking her through the closed window of her smashed car.

She thought briefly before assuring him she was. He then tried the door and also realized it was jammed, so he walked over to the other side and was able to open the passenger door.

Beca slid over to the other side and got out of her car.

Her first concern was for the person who had hit her. She proceeded to ask the small gathering of people if anybody in the other vehicle was hurt. Only then, did the thirty something aged man admit it was him who had hit her. He confessed that he had looked away for only a second, then didn't have enough time to stop before hitting her.

Beca put her hand out and introduced herself. "Hi, I'm Beca Stone."

The man replied, "My name is Jason Crane. I humbly apologize for the trouble I've caused you today."

Instantly she thought Jason was thoughtful and maybe even slightly good looking, so she responded almost too quickly. "I guess if someone is going to mess up my day, it might as well be someone as nice as you." Then she started to blush.

The good news was there were no injuries; the bad news was both vehicles had major damage, plus Beca was really hungry now.

The police were just arriving as she borrowed a cell phone to call her boss, letting him know she would be taking an unscheduled long lunch.

"That should take care of the paperwork," stated the officer.

The EMS people had checked both Jason and Beca for injuries. Both said they would be fine and would seek any additional treatment on their own.

As the wrecker service was loading Beca's car onto the flatbed to be hauled away, Jason looked at her and inquired if he could drive her somewhere, noting his vehicle was still drivable, at least during the daytime.

Beca sputtered sarcastically, "Why would I ride with someone who runs into people?" Then abruptly apologized, saying, "I guess I have foot-in-mouth disease." She thought, *there I go again running my mouth before the brain is engaged.*

"I could use a ride back to work," she commented, "but I was on my way to lunch, which I have not gotten, and I'm starving."

"Well," Jason said, "I can see a fast food restaurant just down the road. Would you let me buy your lunch for the inconvenience I've caused you?"

This time she hesitated and thought carefully, making sure not to embarrass herself again before answering, "I will let you redeem yourself."

Once in the car Beca and Jason sat quietly, both secretly checking the other out, wondering what type of person they were in the company of.

At the restaurant they ordered, then Jason paid just like he said he would. They chose a corner in the far end of the dining area to provide some privacy. Jason didn't see a wedding ring on Beca's hand, which excited him slightly as he was attracted to her. He stuttered slightly, then boldness overtook him as he bluntly asked, "Are you single?" His face turned red as he waited for a reply.

She was startled by the forward question, but did not hesitate answering because she noticed how hard it was for him to ask. She answered softly, "I have never been married."

Jason's heart jumped as he blurted out, "Me either." Then he again tried to apologize for causing the accident, telling her the reason he had looked away for a second was to look at a map. "I live only fifteen miles from here, but I have never come to this area before. My sister just moved over here somewhere, and I was trying to find her place. I'm rambling on, probably boring you."

"No," she answered. "I'm a good listener, and this helps me understand what happened today."

Soon the food disappeared. Beca mentioned that she should get back to work, and that she also had to figure out what to do about her transportation needs. Jason agreed to drop her off at her place of employment, mentioning he too had to do something about his slightly altered vehicle. "I will need your phone number just in case we need to discuss any issues pertaining to the accident," Jason stated, hardly believing the calmness in his voice as he made the self-serving request.

Beca agreed that would be a good idea, and requested his phone number just in case she had an issue.

Back at work she had a lot of explaining to do, the long lunch, some guy dropping her off, and where her car was. Once everybody had heard the story, they repeatedly asked her if she was sure there were no injuries and how could they help her find wheels.

The first thing she did was call the insurance agent to find out if the car was fixable. The only news she got was that it would take a couple days before they would have an answer. So she decided to rent a vehicle until she could make an informed decision. After making a few phone calls and finding a reasonable car to rent, Beca's boss suggested she leave early to get the rental car, even offering to drive her down to pick it up. She was grateful for the great relationship she had with her boss and coworkers.

Once home she quickly realized how stiff her muscles were from the accident, and decided a warm, relaxing bath was just the ticket. After the bath she decided to inform her parents of the eventful day because her mom always worried. As the answering machine kicked in at her parent's house, Beca remembered that they had gone away to Missouri for the week, so she hung up without saying anything.

Missy kept getting under her feet, trying to get attention. Beca was grateful that someone depended on her daily, and somehow the relationship was mutual.

The phone rang and her heart jumped, wondering if it could be Jason. She picked it up just as the doorbell sounded. Her mom was on the phone, so she asked her to hold just a minute as she answered the door. Standing at the door was Jillian who noticed the phone, so she let herself in as only friends could do. After a few minutes of talking with her mom, she hung up and asked Jillian why she had come over. She replied, "James had left his favorite toy, so she had stopped by to pick it up. Then she turned to Beca to ask about the new car in the drive, mentioning, "I didn't even know you were looking for a new ride."

She explained about the accident, and how she had rented a vehicle until the insurance company told her what they would do about her customized Buick. She conveniently left Jason Crane completely out of the conversation, just like she had when talking to her mother just moments ago.

Finally relaxed after the day of unexpected events, Beca sat down at her desk to sort through a few papers. Glancing at the calendar on the wall she momentarily froze. With the childcare weekend, work, and an accident, she had forgotten about her date with Tim tomorrow night. She also realized at that very moment, she didn't even know his last name, or even have a phone number.

The next evening at five minutes before six, Beca thought she heard a motorcycle and quickly confirmed her suspicions by looking out the window. She got rather defensive in her thinking. She reasoned he was inconsiderate, for not informing her ahead of time about the mode of transportation. However she bit her tongue and went out to meet him.

"Nice night!" he shouted as she approached the bike. "Thought I'd bring the two-wheeler, catch some air." He held out a helmet for her to wear.

Expressionless, she took it commenting brashly, "It's a good thing I didn't dress up for this date."

Her attitude eventually mellowed during the non-communication ride that was more enjoyable than she had anticipated. He had chosen a nothing fancy, sit down restaurant for their evening meal together.

During the meal, they both opened up by giving a short synopsis of personal history and explaining who they were individually. Beca even learned his last name was Mann, somehow it seemed to fit him perfectly. She began to relax more as the night progressed.

Alone in her home after Tim had dropped her off, Beca cheerfully reviewed the evening in her mind. Even the part when he had asked if they could spend time together again. She had slightly toyed with his emotions by pretending to evaluate the question, before giving him the answer.

Wednesday the insurance company called, informing Beca they were totaling the car so she could come down to pick up a check. When she bought her Buick, her dad had gone with her, but her parents were out of town this week. She decided it was time to stand on her own feet and made plans to go car shopping alone that evening. Being money conscious and not wanting payments again, she decided to spend only up to as much as the check was on a gently used vehicle. This was an unexpected expense and presently she didn't have extra money to put with it.

The night flew by as Beca went from car lot to car lot. She wanted a car to fit her personality, that meant comfortable, dependable—nothing flashy. After a few hours of looking, she headed home frustrated that she had found nothing suitable for her needs. When she entered the door at home she immediately noticed the flashing light on the answering machine.

A NEW CAR

Beca hit the play button on the blinking answering machine, only to hear her friend Rhonda telling her to call as soon as possible. Jillian had told her about the accident, and she wanted to express her concern.

After all the details were explained, Rhonda reminded Beca to call if she needed any help looking for a new car. Then she stammered, "As your friend I want to give you a heads up. Rhonda gave that single guy we met at the campground your phone number."

Beca fell silent, not wanting to divulge any knowledge of the conspiracy. "Is that right?" she finally responded as if she knew nothing. "Thanks for the info, and don't worry, I won't rat you out."

Thursday flew by because work was busy, it seemed all the contractors were stocking up for big projects. Just before leaving, she decided to look on the Internet for a used vehicle. Scrolling down through the listings, she found a couple of cars that might just work for her. She jotted down the numbers and addresses before heading home.

After dinner Beca called on the two cars she found on the Internet, one was already sold and the other, a Nissan, was about ten miles away, but it sounded interesting. *Well*, she thought, *it's a nice night for a ride, and it should be light for a couple more hours, so maybe I'll go take a look at the car.*

When she pulled into the drive along side of the Nissan, a twenty-something-year-old man came out of the house and answered all the questions she had about the car.

"Can I take it for a spin?" she inquired from the man who had introduced himself as Peter Bell.

"Only if you tell me your name," Peter said.

Suddenly she felt embarrassed for forgetting her manners. She thrust her hand out toward Peter and shyly answered, "My name is Beca Stone."

Peter replied, "If it's all right with you, I would like to ride along."

Once everything was adjusted for comfort, they eased out onto the road. Peter didn't say a word, he just sat like he was with an old friend where communication wasn't a requirement, but it made her rather uncomfortable. "It has a lot of power," she stated, trying to indulge in small talk to ease the tension she felt. Then she asked, "Why are you selling it?"

Peter's deadpan answer floored Beca as he stated, "It was my wife's car, she passed away a couple of months ago, and I don't need two cars."

It left a heavy awkward silence, and now she wished he had not come along for the ride. Peter noticed she had tensed up and quickly apologized for causing an embarrassing situation, then briefly mentioned that he had really loved his wife, Linda, and missed her greatly.

Back at Peter's home, Beca walked around the car again.

Peter said, "I can see you really like the car, so make me an offer I can't refuse. I think you and the car look good together."

Beca had to admit, she did like the way the car handled, and it was her style of comfort without being flashy. "I need time to think about it. Can I call you tomorrow with an offer?"

"Well," Peter said, "I can appreciate that. You already have my phone number so I will look forward to hearing from you tomorrow." He then added, "Thanks for coming out and enjoy the rest of the evening, Beca."

She felt a shiver when he said her name, even if it was still over seventy degrees out. She gave Peter a smile as she slipped back into the rental car, and slowly pulled onto the road toward home.

Driving home, Beca's thoughts wandered as she reminisced about the accident that had interrupted her monotonous life. She smiled slightly when she realized that in the last week, she had met two more good-looking single guys. She reprimanded herself for thinking such a bold thought, especially since Peter had just lost his wife a couple of months ago. Not only that, but she just had a date with Tim Mann, who seemed interested in her.

Somehow she knew life was going to be a little more interesting from now on, and the best part was, it was her own little secret. She had kept from telling her friends, maybe out of fear that things would be forever the same, or maybe it was the excitement of having a secret. *How did I get here so quickly?* Beca wondered, suddenly aware of pulling into her own driveway. *I must have been lost in my thoughts.*

The answering machine was blinking again as Beca entered the door. It was her mom asking if she had remembered to check on their house while they were gone that week, then she informed her they planned on being home Sunday afternoon. Missy greeted her with the customary leg rub, letting her know she was grateful to have her home. Beca did some checking on the value of the Nissan she had just looked at and decided to make Peter an offer the next day.

After work on Friday, Beca hurried home so she could call Peter with the offer she came up with for the Nissan. After some negotiation, they came to an agreement with plans for her to pick the car up Saturday morning.

Hanging up the phone, she immediately called Rhonda to see if her friend could pick her up, and bring her to Peter's house to get her new car the next day. Rhonda said she would be happy to help, and suggested they go out for breakfast on the way. Beca decided to keep the rental through the weekend, so she had time to transfer the insurance and license from the Buick to the Nissan.

Saturday was one of those glorious bright sun-shining, laid back, quiet days, that boost everybody's spirits, and Beca was already excited with the prospect of getting her new ride. Rhonda arrived, and because Beca was so excited, the car had hardly stopped before she was already jumping in.

"Wow!" exclaimed Rhonda. "You must have been watching from the doorway. You have all day you know, but I guess I would probably be just like you if it were me. It's always fun to have a change of pace or something new to look forward to."

The two friends headed to the restaurant for breakfast. Rhonda shared how busy her children, Graham and Christine, had been keeping her. She also indicated how she appreciated going out with Beca for the morning, giving her a break because the kids really seemed wound up this week. She continued thinking out loud, saying, "Maybe I need to give them more responsibilities around the house, maybe that would keep them occupied during the summer break."

At the restaurant, Beca let slip that the guy she was buying the car from was single, but hastily added, "He's really too young for me."

Rhonda raised her eyebrows, leaned forward, and looked right into her friend's eyes. "I think I see a glimmer of interest. Are you being honest with your friend who knows you very, very well?"

Immediately Beca felt her face grow warm as she blushed. "This coffee is really warm," she said as she grabbed her napkin to wipe her face, trying desperately to hide her emotions. Finally regaining her composure, Beca retaliated. "Rhonda, Rhonda, I told you Peter was too young for me; besides I don't even know the guy, so don't jump to conclusions."

Rhonda apologized for being so forward, sat back, and then deadpanned, "Well, I guess when we get the car we will see just how young and good looking Peter really is, and how you act around him."

Beca had nothing more to say at that point and quickly changed the topic by saying, "The breakfast was good while it lasted. Oh, I almost forgot, we need to stop at the bank to get a cashier's check for the car on the way."

En route to pick up the car, Rhonda candidly asked, "So have there been any guys calling you lately?"

Beca knew exactly what her nosy friend was inquiring, but didn't feel like divulging any information that might give her satisfaction. So, she lied, "I can't imagine why one would, not much ever happens in my life."

The car was sitting up by the house when the two girls arrived at Peter's home. Rhonda made a comment that it was a sharp-looking vehicle, stating that Beca would look good in it. They did not see any activity around the house, so Beca went to the door to ring the bell. After ringing the bell, it seemed to take forever for Peter to answer. She was relieved and happy he was home, thankful that she didn't need to return at a later time.

Peter stepped outside, and a little girl followed him. Beca was slightly stunned as Peter explained, "Sorry for the delay in getting out here. We were just finishing our breakfast dishes and had to dry our hands." Then he motioned toward the dark-haired little girl and introduced her as his beautiful daughter, Ruth. "She is four years old," he stated with a proud smile. Then he looked at his daughter, and told her to go back in the house and play until Daddy was done selling Mommy's car. The child quickly complied.

"She is so cute," both Rhonda and Beca said, almost at the same time.

Peter smiled slightly as a glow spread across his face, and he said, "Yes, she is. She looks just like my late wife."

Rhonda could see by the expression on his face that he really missed his wife and could hear in his voice the tenderness he must have had for her.

"Did you bring the money?" Peter asked, bringing her back to reality.

"Ah, yes," she babbled as she handed Peter the cashier's check for the agreed amount.

Peter continued to look directly at Beca as he handed her the keys and title and said, "You made a good investment. I'm sure the car will be good to you."

Both Peter and Beca said "thank you" to the other, then stood there in an awkward manner.

Rhonda took the lead by saying, "If I'm not needed here anymore, I think I'll head back."

Beca answered, "You can head back to my house for a little while if you want. Then I can show you the car a little more."

Rhonda agreed and left as Beca was sliding into the driver's seat of the Nissan.

Back home, she parked the car as Rhonda came over with a grin that could only mean one thing from a friend. "You like him don't you?" She wasted no words giving her own opinion. "He looks young, but I'll bet he's closer in age than you might expect, and any girl would think he was a great catch for looks."

Beca ignored Rhonda's bold approach and calmly asked, "So what do think of my new car?"

The two friends just looked at each other briefly, each wondering which conversation was going to take precedence. Finally Rhonda turned toward the car and said, "Let's get a good look at your new set of wheels" as she slipped into the driver's seat. Beca was smiling as she stated, "It really drives nice. I think it's the right car for me."

After briefly looking the car over, Rhonda mentioned she needed to get back home because her family was going to the beach for the afternoon, and she still had a few things to do before going. "Why don't you stop over for lunch tomorrow?" Rhonda asked. "I think you need a break after the week you've had."

Beca agreed. She again thanked Rhonda for helping her pick up the car, and told her to enjoy the beach with her family.

Beca had been so busy the whole week, due to the accident and all the issues that went with it, she had neglected checking on her parent's house. Hopping into the rental car, wishing she could be driving the Nissan, Beca headed to her parents' home to take care of a few things there, before they returned tomorrow.

Everything was fine at the house, except that the lawn needed mowing. So, Beca got out the mower and proceeded to clean up the yard. It really didn't take that long, but it was warm out, and having been in overdrive all morning, she was really tired when she finished the lawn. She headed home to get some lunch and take it easy. On the ride home she was thinking to herself, *I want to put my CDs in my new car and play with the stereo.*

Beca enjoyed the warm afternoon, checking out all the details of her new car, while playing with all the different controls. She even washed the car, soaking in the warm sunshine and working on her tan at the same time. Her stomach told her it must be dinnertime, so she parked the car in the garage until she could get the license and insurance taken care of on Monday. She then went in the house to feed Missy and take a shower, before heading out to do some grocery shopping.

Sunday was a carbon copy of Saturday, thought Beca as she dressed for church, thinking it was a beautiful day for her parents to drive home. After church Beca drove to Rhonda's house for lunch. Her friends often liked to include her in their families, and she enjoyed being with them. Rhonda's children, Graham and Christine, were always excited to see their honorary aunt.

Today was no different as they both talked non-stop about yesterday's outing at the beach. Graham, being the older one, bragged about how he could swim farther into the deep area than his sister, Christine. But she had her own bragging rights, saying when they built sand castles, hers was bigger than his, even if her father had helped.

Lunch was grilled chicken, which reminded Beca of the camping trip that the three friends had taken just a few weeks earlier. The conversation turned to the adventures that the girls had when camping, filling Rhonda's family in on all the details she may have purposefully missed telling them earlier. Beca was grateful that the subject of the three men visiting their campfire never came up.

The lunch went fast as the stories seemed slightly embellished, making whoever was telling it the seasoned camper, keeping them all in stitches. Beca sighed as the conversation subsided, then stated, "That was really good, but I still think anything tastes better over a campfire."

Rhonda's family all agreed.

Beca waved good-bye to Rhonda and her family as she headed back home in her rental car, saying out loud to the vehicle, "Tomorrow you go back to your home, and I get to start driving my new wheels." A smile spread across her face as she recollected the events of the past week, especially how the bad had brought some good. She was hoping that having met a couple of new single guys could bring something good to her future.

Beca's mom called in the early evening to inform her they had gotten back home without any issues, and also thanking her for mowing the lawn. She informed her mom she had bought a Nissan to replace the Buick, and asked if dad could meet her at the car rental place after work for a ride back home. "Besides," she added, "I really want dad to see my new car."

"I think we will both come to pick you up, then I can see it too," her mom replied.

Beca left work a half hour early because the car rental place closed the same time they did. She finished the necessary paperwork just as her parents drove in. "Nice timing," Beca said as she got in the back of her parents minivan.

Mom looked back at her and asked, "Are you hungry? Dad and I thought we would take you out to eat on the way back to your place. We can tell you about our trip to Branson, and you can tell us about your accident."

"Well, it looks like I'm at your mercy," she stated from the back seat.

Her mother turned back to her dad, saying, "Let's try the steak house tonight, Josh."

After ordering, the conversation drifted to the different shows that Beca's parents had seen while in Branson. Sometimes they got so excited they were both talking at the same time, but Beca was happy her parents were able to have made the trip creating memories together. "Wow!" exclaimed Elaine, while they were finishing their desserts. "I can't believe the time has flown by so quickly."

"Beca, oh Beca," she said with compassion only a mother could have. "We haven't even given you a chance to talk about all the events of your week, with the accident, and finding a new vehicle. We feel bad having not been here for you in a time of crisis."

Beca suggested they head toward her house, so she could show them her new ride, and she could fill them in on the details during the drive. It seemed all the details had been told, except she had conveniently left out any indication of interest, in meeting the two males involved in the accident or buying of the new car. Besides, at thirty-two years of age, she had enough of life's experiences to know when not to jump to conclusions, or give opportunity for her family and friends to jump to conclusions at her expense.

At her home, Beca suggested she back the Nissan out of the garage so her parents could get a proper look at the car. Her mom mentioned she really liked the silver color to which dad said, "Doesn't really matter what it looks like if it gets good gas mileage and is reliable."

Beca heard her mother mutter under her breath, "Men are always thinking of the practical, but everybody knows first impressions matter." After a few minutes, both her parents gave their approval, mentioning the car was a good fit for her.

Alone at last for the evening, Beca fed Missy who was always happy to see her. She actually liked being alone at times, enjoying the peace and quiet so she could read; other times she liked to crank the music up, bothering nobody if she sang along. Music was something she had always enjoyed and when she had looked at the Nissan, one of the first things she had checked for was if it had a good stereo with a CD player.

A full week passed before life had finally gotten back to its normal pace. Beca was enjoying the summer weather and certainly enjoyed driving her new car. The job was going well, and she occasionally did things with her friends and visited her parents. She had grown accustomed and was content with how full her life was, even without some of the expectations she had as a young girl.

It had been so busy the past couple of weeks that she had gotten only a few short bike rides in. On Thursday evening there was nothing pressing, so after doing the dishes from her evening meal, she retrieved her bike from the garage. The weather was warm, so she made sure her water bottle was full before starting out. It felt so good to feel the warm breeze and to smell nature.

These jaunts kept her familiar with the neighborhood and beyond. Tonight she rode for almost two hours, which—according to her speedometer—covered about twenty miles. It was a workout and entertainment all at the same time. It also gave her time to think about her life. Today while riding, she began to wonder why Tim had not called for another date. Was she over anxious? Was he really interested? Did he think the driving distance was too much hassle?

Finally after driving herself crazy by running through all the possible scenarios, she made up her mind to accept whatever happened in the uncommitted hardly even a relationship. The shower that evening was not only desired, but needed after such a satisfying and stress relieving ride on the warm summer evening.

Friday night Beca took care of the yard work because the weather forecast indicated rain on Saturday. It had been nice all week, and now that the weekend was here, the weather didn't want to cooperate for any outdoor activities. It worked well with her to do the yard on Friday and the housework on Saturday. *Besides*, she reasoned, *I need to go do some shopping, and rainy weather gives me an excuse.*

When Beca got out of the shower, the answering machine was blinking. Her first thought was, *now who wants me to watch their kids so they can enjoy time together?* She hit the play button then stood dumfounded as she heard, "Hi, Beca. This is ah… Jason Crane, the a rude guy who a wasn't a careful driver and hit your car a couple weeks ago. I've been doing a some a thinking lately, about you I mean, and I ah…just thought maybe we could ah…get together if a if you would like. Sorry, I a missed you, but maybe it's like easier for both of us if I just talk to the answering machine. Please give me a call if you have any interest, my number is 555-2143. Bye."

Beca just stood looking at the machine for a few seconds, then played it again to be sure she had heard correctly.

CHANGES

Yes, she had heard right; Jason had left her a message on the answering machine, and he sounded rather nervous. What did she know about this guy? She did like the way he looked, and he did seem like a man of compassion, but was this a door of opportunity or another disappointment? *Don't make a quick decision*, she warned herself. She decided to make a bowl of popcorn, watch some television, and take time to do some thinking. The microwave was beeping, indicating the popcorn was done, when the phone suddenly rang. Thoughts of who it might be ran through her head as she picked up the phone and answered with a cheerful "Hi." Relief came as she recognized her friend Jillian's voice.

Her reaction to the cheerful "Hi" was immediate as she commented, "Someone's in a good mood tonight, are they not?"

"Well," Beca replied almost too quickly, "I'm just happy I got all my outside work done before the rain comes tomorrow. I was just sitting down with a bowl of warm popcorn. You know how I love my popcorn," she added, hoping to deter more questions.

"Yes, you do," Jillian replied, then mentioned she had called because they had not talked in a couple of weeks and needed to catch up. She suggested Beca join her family next Friday night, for dinner and campfire at the campground. Jillian's family was going camping for the upcoming Fourth of July weekend. Beca agreed it was a good idea, indicating she had nothing else on the agenda, so they made tentative plans for next Friday evening. Jillian was going to call later to both confirm, and discuss any food items she may need to bring.

Then from who knows where, Jillian had the audacity to inquire if she had any guys call her lately. Startled, Beca was speechless. Jillian quickly realized the awkwardness of the situation and smoothed it over by changing the subject. She began telling Beca what James had been doing lately. The conversation eventually dwindled and both said "good-bye."

Hanging up the phone, Beca said to herself, *I should have let the answering machine get that. I like my friends, but now my popcorn is cold, and I haven't even had time to think about the phone call from Jason yet.*

Suddenly, all reason left Beca as she spontaneously picked up the receiver and dialed Jason's number. Speaking to the phone, she boldly said, "It's time I started taking chances."

Jason answered on the second ring, which made her wonder if he had caller ID. Maybe he was waiting for her call, but right now that didn't seem to matter. "Jason," she said. "It's Beca, Beca Stone. I called to let you know that maybe we could get together sometime if you'd like."

Jason didn't waste any time or words as he suggested they go out for breakfast tomorrow morning.

She took a few seconds to think it over, remembering it was going to rain tomorrow and she had already taken care of most of her weekend work.

Jason, intimidated by the brief silence, apologized and stated that maybe some other time might be better.

"Tomorrow morning works good for me," Beca finally stated.

They agreed to meet at a local restaurant at eight the next morning, then said "good-bye."

Saturday Beca woke to the sound of rain hitting the window. Suddenly she remembered she had a breakfast date. *A date, is that what this was?* Why hadn't that thought crossed her mind? Glancing at the clock she felt all the blood quickly draining from her body, the clock said 7:50. Jumping from the bed quickly, she mentally scolded herself for not setting the alarm as she hurried to fix the dreaded morning look. Beca didn't like being late for things. But worse than being late was looking like she had just crawled from under something; she did have her limits.

Jumping in the car, she was already almost ten minutes late. It was a good thing the restaurant they had picked was close. In the back of her mind, Beca wondered if Jason had gotten past first impressions and would not count this against her for any future relationship possibilities. The rain didn't seem to slow her down, although it should have, it wasn't that long ago she was in an accident.

Beca checked her watch quickly as she entered the restaurant. Twenty minutes late; well, she was going to find out right away if Jason was patient and understanding. Looking around the restaurant, she did not see him and wondered if she may have forgotten what he looked like in just a few weeks.

She looked up just as Jason was approaching her from inside the restaurant saying, "I thought you had changed your mind, and I was drowning myself in decaf coffee."

Beca laughed at his sense of humor, then turned sympathetic and apologized, trying to explain about not setting the alarm. She also mentioned how she had just thrown herself together in a rush, trying to get there as soon as possible.

Jason quickly forgave her, saying he understood that being single sometimes gives freedoms we take for granted when there is nobody to set our schedules for. Then he gave her a compliment saying, "Had you not told me you had been thrown together this morning, I would have never known." Then he hesitated before concluding, "You look great."

The waitress showed up just then, so they placed their orders. They both sighed as they sat back and started sipping their coffee. Jason's sigh was because Beca had shown up, while hers was from the hurriedness and his understanding attitude.

"I have to admit," Jason spoke, "I'm really out of my comfort zone, so if I seem awkward or nervous, it's because I am." Looking sheepishly into her eyes he continued, "I really want to know who Beca Stone is, so please tell me all about yourself. Who you are, what you do, what your hobbies are, about your family. I want to know it all." Then he hesitated, "I'm sorry for rambling on, please, you talk."

Beca, being slightly reserved, thought to herself, *I'm not revealing everything. I don't know much about him either. We have only talked for maybe about half an hour before today.* So she started telling him about the generic parts of her life, like the house she owned and the fact that she actually liked doing yard work.

The waitress came with the food, so between bites they both shared parts of who they were. Beca mentioning her love of bicycling and how she actually liked to crank up her music. Jason stated he had just one sister, Emily, whose house he was trying to find, when he ran into the back of her car a few weeks ago. "By the way, I did find her house," he said, "but not until a couple of days later, due to our unscheduled meeting."

Beca had two things she really wanted to find out about Jason, and through the conversations Jason answered them both without her even needing to ask. He was thirty-four years old, actually only fourteen months older than she was, and he had never married because—according to him—he buried himself in books to hide his shyness. After high school, college had been the priority then a career was the focus, therefore, leaving no time for any relationship. Now, he told her he realized his priorities might have been misplaced. Jason said his hobbies were reading and hiking—which seems ironic, as one is hardly any movement, and the other, a lot—but then a couple of her own hobbies were similar like reading and biking. Maybe they were a lot alike in subtle ways.

The food had been gone for almost half an hour, and neither of them could drink another cup of coffee. Looking around the restaurant, Jason suggested they let other patrons have their table. As he picked up the check, Beca said, "I can pay my own way."

Jason quickly and boldly stated, "I believe I asked you out for breakfast."

She softly answered, "Yes, you did. Thank you."

The softness in her voice melted Jason's heart; he was just beginning to see who she was and was both enticed and attracted.

When they reached the exit, Jason nervously asked, "Is there any chance we could spend time together again?" His heart was in his throat, knowing this relationship was at the point of starting or ending, depending on her answer.

Beca turned and looked at him for a couple of seconds without talking, only adding to his tension, before she cautiously answered, "I would like that."

She left the restaurant lighthearted, despite the dreariness of the day. Shopping was what she had planned the evening before, and that was exactly what she was going to do.

The day flew as Beca shopped at multiple stores, including getting a few needed groceries. At the grocery store, she had stopped at the deli to pick up an early evening meal to eat at home. Somehow in the excitement of the day with breakfast out, followed by shopping, she had forgotten lunch and was now tired. The deli was a welcomed convenience.

At home the first thing she noticed, was the answering machine blinking. Thinking to herself, *there sure has been a lot of activity in life since the auto accident.* Was it really an accident or an incident? Was Jason calling already? It really was too soon. She didn't want someone that was pushy or desperate in her life. Then she began to wonder if others thought she may be that way, and she shuttered at the thought. The message was from Jillian, to which Beca breathed a sigh of relief. She had called only to confirm Friday night at the campground, asking her to bring supplies for s'mores to the campfire, adding "Bring plenty. There may be some extra visitors."

Beca promptly called back confirming she had gotten the message, and agreed to bring the goods.

Sunday morning before church, Elaine Stone called her daughter, asking her to join them for lunch. She informed her that her brother Jake and his family were coming over for an afternoon visit. Jake lived about seventy-five miles away, so the visits were infrequent but always welcomed. Her mother commented, "I know it's a rather short notice, but the plans were made late last night, so I understand if you can't make it, but Jake really wants to see his big sister."

Beca didn't hesitate in her answer as she enjoyed Jake and his family, not to mention she had a new car to show off.

When Jake and his wife, Kris, arrived, the house came alive as their three boys—Carl age six, Brad age five, and Robert age three—were sick of riding and had energy to burn. Grandma Elaine was always happy to see her babies, even if they temporally wore her out.

Jake gave his sister a hug, as was the family custom when greeting. Beca enjoyed the hugs from each of her nephews and the cute way they said her name. They hardly had time for the greetings, before the announcement that dinner was ready. It took no further urging to get the family seated at the table.

Eight people around the table made it lively as the food disappeared and multiple conversations thrived. Just as Elaine asked if anybody saved room for desert, Jake cleared his throat and announced they were expecting their fourth child. When the shock wore off the adults, they smiled and congratulated them, asking when the addition was expected. Kris replied, "The due date is December 14, just in time for Christmas."

"And just in time for another tax deduction," Jake added, causing everybody to laugh. "Well," stated Jake, "that's the reason we wanted to visit today, so we could tell you the happy news in person."

Nobody said anything to Beca, but she suddenly felt the personal pressure of being single and childless. As happy as she was for her brother and his wife, the pain cut deep. She knew her family members cared about her feelings and loved her unconditionally, and that they would never purposely do or say anything to hurt her emotionally. She rebuked herself for allowing the negative thoughts and envy that crept in.

Dessert was served, and Beca joined in the happy celebration thinking, *I've actually had a couple of dates recently, maybe there is hope.* She was not ready to share any secrets with her family at this time, just like Jake and Kris had not shared about the baby for a few months.

After dinner, she showed off her new ride to Jake and Kris, then went into all the details of why she needed a new car. She was careful not to mention Jason Crane, other than he was just the guy who had run into her.

Jake approved of her vehicle choice, saying with a smirk as only a brother could, "I'll bet heads will be turning to check out the chick in this hot car."

The three nephews sure loved their aunt Beca, and she loved them just as much. Sometimes she wished they lived closer, but she understood Jake took his job as a real estate appraiser when and where it was available many years ago. He really loved the job, and it was working well for him and his family.

It seemed just a couple of hours later when Kris reminded Jake that they had over an hour drive, and it was already early evening. So everybody said their good-byes and they parted ways.

The next couple of days were uneventful for Beca, until she came home on Wednesday and got her mail. In the mail was a letter with the return address of Peter Bell, the guy she had bought her car from. Her heart leaped when she saw the address, but scolded herself saying out loud, "Calm down, you don't even know what the letter is about."

NOW WHAT?

Once inside the house, Beca had only one thing on her mind: opening the letter from Peter Bell because the curiosity of what it contained was overwhelming. However, it seemed Missy was feeling playful after being home alone all day and kept getting under Beca's feet. Realizing there would be no peace in the house for the moment, she got some food out for Missy and gave her the few moments of attention desired.

After Missy settled down, Beca opened the letter. Peter simply stated that he regretted he had taken the spare tire out of the car when cleaning it, and had forgotten to put it back. He asked if she could please call him to collect it; he had lost her phone number, thus explaining the reason for the letter. Her first thought was, *what if I would have had a flat*, her blood pressure rising slightly at his inconsiderate mistake. "I want my tire," she said aloud in a demanding way, to her empty house.

Then she realized Peter didn't even have to tell her about the tire, she never even knew it was missing. Maybe she should give this guy a break—he was being somewhat considerate. She tossed the letter aside, *thinking I'll give him a call later*, and started preparing her evening meal.

After dinner Beca retrieved the letter and gave Peter a call. It worked well for both if she came directly after work, arriving between 5:15 and 5:30 in the evening. Thursday was another one of those "I can't keep up" days at work. Maybe because the Fourth of July weekend was almost here and everybody was taking Monday off, so she was tired when 5:00 p.m. arrived. *Good*, she thought, *I have only one thing I need to do tonight before I can relax*. So she headed to Peter's house to pick up the spare tire.

Meeting Peter again stirred something in her that both excited and bothered her. She remembered he had sold her the car because his wife had passed away a few months ago. How could she have thoughts or feelings on the situation? She knew it was taboo for anybody to be thinking of a new relationship so soon, besides didn't she just have a date with another guy less than a week ago? Her mind was playing many scenarios, so she shook her head, trying to focus on the present. It had been a few weeks, and now seeing Peter again reminded her of the initial meeting—his good looks and the compassion in his voice, not to mention his cute daughter, Ruth, and the tenderness he had shown toward her.

Peter tossed the tire in the trunk for Beca, apologizing for the inconvenience, mentioning that he sent the letter because he wanted to make it right. After small talk and again meeting his daughter, Ruth, Beca boldly handed Peter her phone number. She suggested he put it in a safe place for a while just in case something else came up. Then thanked him for making it right, before wishing him a happy Fourth of July and saying "good-bye."

On the way home her mind again began to wander, "What are you thinking?" she spoke out loud. Was that forward, brave, or just plain rude, giving him the phone number? Was she expecting something that couldn't be? It was a legitimate excuse—he contacted her first. *He's too young for me, and he's not interested in a relationship at this point. Besides, I did have a date with two other men recently, so I'm not really interested, am I? Why are you thinking like this? You know it's not reality,* she scolded herself.

Having been so deep in thought, she wondered how she had gotten home so quickly. She abruptly decided to leave the car out so she could wash it after dinner, realizing just how nice the day really was. It seemed the last hour had reenergized her, maybe that was due to the change of pace or maybe there were other reasons, but none of that seemed to matter at the moment.

The store shut down early on Friday, even though the Fourth of July holiday was on Monday. It allowed the employees where Beca worked a head start on the holiday weekend, so Beca was home by three in the afternoon. She was excited about visiting Jillian's family at the campsite, and she looked forward to seeing James, her honorary adopted nephew.

Quickly changing clothes and packing a sweatshirt for later—certain that nobody minded if she showed up early—she grabbed the supply of graham crackers, marshmallows, and chocolate bars for the s'mores she had agreed to, before heading out.

When she arrived at the campground, she remembered Jillian had not told her what site they would be on. She had never wanted a cell phone, she had considered them an unnecessary expense, but at times like this she thought one sure would come in handy. She just started driving around, hoping to recognize people or equipment. Thankfully it was not a big campground, and in just a few minutes she spotted Jillian, who was setting up her tent with her husband, Chad.

No sooner had she parked when James came running over to her shouting, "Auntie Beca! Auntie Beca, come see what I found!"

She waved hello to Chad and Jillian then obediently followed James to some weeds at the sites edge. "What could be so interesting?" she asked James, who couldn't contain himself any longer.

"There"—he pointed to a hole in the ground—"I saw a rat go in that hole!"

Beca laughed as she looked over at Chad who also seemed amused by his child's perception.

"James," she said, "I think it was probably a chipmunk, and that's his home; he lives under ground."

"Well," replied James as he crossed his arms in defiance. "It looked like a rat to me."

Beca asked if she could help with the site setup, so Jillian gladly gave her the assignment of unloading the firewood and placing chairs around the pit. Chad piped in that maybe James could give a hand, which everybody knew was just a way of keeping him on the site more than it was keeping him busy.

However, James had other ideas. With so much to explore, he was soon in the next site asking an older couple questions like, "What's your name? Did you see the rat? Do you live here? Are you going to have a fire tonight?"

Chad quietly apologized to the couple for the intruder and led James back to their site, suggesting he help get the beds ready for that night.

Soon the campfire was started; the evening meal was to be the classic hot dog roast over the open fire, with potato salad and Jell-o to round off the meal. Roasting hotdogs and smelling the wood fire while watching other campers, created an air of excitement for all to enjoy.

Suddenly Beca turned to Jillian and asked, "Didn't you tell me to bring plenty of s'more stuff because there may be other people here? Someone else better be coming, otherwise I'll probably eat more s'mores than I ought to, just so they don't go to waste." Then she eyed her friend meaningfully. "You better not be trying to set me up!"

Jillian replied, "Of course not. I invited Rhonda and her family to join in the evening campfire. I wanted it to be a surprise. You know how I like to keep life interesting. They should be here in about an hour, giving us time to finish eating, maybe we can even squeeze a short walk in before they come."

With cleanup done, Beca suggested just she and Jillian go for that walk mentioned previously.

Chad replied, "Go for it, girls. James and I will keep the fire going."

The two friends walked through the campground, admiring other campers with their setups, even making comments about how some people were novice campers, and others just didn't appear to have a clue. When they arrived back at Jillian's camp site, they found Rhonda and her family had already arrived with their two children, Graham and Christine, who were poking around at the fire.

Smiles and hugs followed as the three friends got reacquainted, momentarily ignoring the men and children. Soon the entire group of eight was sitting around the campfire. The guys started discussing summer vacations and work. The kids were laughing as they threw pinecones in the fire—watching the flames leap up as the cones glowed brightly. It would still be light for a little while—at this time of the year—but the temperature was already dropping. Evening was approaching as the sun dove behind the trees, so the fire was a warm welcome.

Rhonda sat quietly, just looking at Beca. When she made eye contact with Beca, whom she had not seen recently, she asked a bold question. "So has there been any contact with that Peter guy since you bought the car from him? Or some other guy we might need to know about?"

The others got suddenly quiet, even the kids listened as the question hung in the awkward silence.

Beca looked at Jillian then back at Rhonda, dumfounded and caught off guard. She remembered Rhonda had gone with her to pick up the car and knew an answer was expected. "He had a spare tire for the car I had to go back to pick up," she deadpanned. "Sorry, no other guys to report at this time." Then she quickly changed the subject by suggesting it was time for those s'mores. She was not giving any more information than necessary, especially in a group setting.

Saturday Beca slept in as the day dawned overcast but warm and dry. She had made arrangements with her dad to install a bike rack on the Nissan, hoping in the future to explore new areas with her bike.

By late morning she arrived at her parents' home. Her dad was just putting the lawn mower away, so they went in the house together. Mom was just getting their morning coffee ready and insisted Beca join them and then informed her they expected her to stay for lunch. After coffee, both father and daughter worked on the bike rack installation, while Beca filled her dad in on the latest saga pertaining to the campground outing.

She enjoyed these special times with her father and took this opportunity to say, "Dad, I'm very thankful for the relationship we have, and there will always be a special place in my heart for you." Then she gave him a hug, again thanking him for helping with the bike rack. After lunch Beca said "good-bye," mentioning she had to get home to try the new rack out.

She had barely entered the house, when the phone rang. Hurriedly picking it up as an intrusion to her plans, she answered, hoping whoever it was didn't desire to talk long. The caller introduced himself as Tim Mann, causing her to quickly forget any immediate plans she had.

He apologized for the length of time between their date and finally calling again, explaining he had not forgotten her but made the excuse of how life sometimes is just busy. He got right to the point by asking her if he could make arrangements for another dinner date with her the following weekend. She was enticed by his candor, and they set a pickup time of six for the next Saturday evening. He also made a promise to leave the bike home, picking her up in something with four wheels this time.

Finally Beca had her bike on the rack mounted to her car, her music playing loudly, and—with windows down—she sped toward the rails to trails riding area about twenty miles from her home. She had seen the trail many times but just never had the opportunity to explore it, and today was her chance.

She had been on the trail about an hour, still headed away from her car when the sky began to darken. *It wasn't supposed to rain today*, she thought, *but I better head back just in case*. Half an hour later, Beca realized it was going to rain, and she was going to get wet regardless of how fast she peddled.

The rain started slowly when she had only about a mile to go, but she was soaked in short order. What happened next happened so quickly, she only remembered looking up at the rain coming down. Apparently, she had hit a pothole filled with water, so it was unnoticeable. She had lost control and wiped out.

Now she was thankful for the precaution of wearing a helmet, but it had not protected her whole body. She had multiple scrapes and felt a sharp pain in her left wrist. She struggled getting to her feet while looking around to see if there was anybody nearby, but everybody else had deserted the trail because of the rain.

Beca took a quick inspection of her bike and groaned as she noticed the front wheel was slightly bent. It prevented her from riding it, which she had hoped she could still do, even if her arm did hurt. She disconnected the brake on the front wheel, allowing it to turn without getting stuck—due to the bent rim—before walking the bike back to the car in the now steady rain. This was not the day she had pictured when she woke that holiday weekend morning.

After securing the bike on the rack, Beca headed to the hospital to have her arm checked out. The prognosis was better than she thought it might be. The doctor informed her it was only a very badly sprained wrist, which should be better in a few days to a week.

Good thing I'm right handed, she thought, but knew it could still be a challenge. At least with the holiday weekend she was off work for a few days. Now she hoped it would heal enough to be useful on Tuesday, otherwise this would be an unscheduled extended weekend.

With the scrapes bruises and wrist bandaged up, Beca headed home to recuperate; that was about all the excitement she could handle today, and maybe for the weekend.

Sunday morning at church, Elaine Stone immediately noticed the scrapes and wrapped arm on her daughter. She quickly made her way over, and, with a look of concern promptly asked, "What happened now? Did you have another car accident?"

Beca knew this was going to happen. She noticed Lisa and a few more of her friends approaching, along with her father.

"I'm okay," she explained to the small group. "I just took a small spill on my bike yesterday." Then she added, "My bike also has a few injuries. I'll probably need to purchase a whole new rim for it because it was bent up in the mishap." She explained her wrist was only a sprain and not broken and the other injuries were minor.

Her mother sighed, "Thank you, Lord," loud enough for everybody nearby to hear.

After church, Beca's mom asked her if she still planned to spend tomorrow, the Fourth of July, with them as was the tradition. Jake and Kris were coming for the annual backyard barbeque, she reminded her. She was not one to be intimidated by her minor inconvenience and certainly didn't want to disappoint her parents. Giving a stern look, she boldly stated, "Of course, Mom. Nothing has changed, and I don't want any special treatment either."

Monday proved to be a picture perfect day. With clear skies, the temperature was already in the low seventies by early morning, with predictions of mid eighties later in the day. Beca looked forward to the annual barbeque, which always took place in the early afternoon. The time between the parade and the cookout was reserved for the art fairs in town. Her brother, Jake, and his family would not be able to watch the parade with them but promised to be there for the cookout.

At the cookout each year, a friendly Frisbee golf competition took place with her family. This year Jake enjoyed mocking Beca—even though she competed, he kept calling her a lame duck. The lame duck didn't win the game but placed better than Jake did, allowing her to return the mockery by letting him know, that he had been beaten by a wounded girl. Jake just laughed and hugged his sister.

Tuesday Beca called into work and explained the sprained wrist, saying she thought it best if it were given at least another day of recovery but promised to be back on Wednesday. A couple of hours later she turned her attention to getting the bike repaired. Removing the front rim, she headed to the cycle shop to purchase a new one and have them transfer the rubber from the old one. Once back home and the bike reassembled, she was satisfied with the results but thought it best to hold off riding until she fully mended.

Back to work on Wednesday, Beca found it hard to keep up, as the left hand was still weak and sore. Her boss and coworkers were patient and understanding, so the day went well all things considered.

Finally, the weekend arrived and she was looking forward to the date with Tim on Saturday. She kept herself busy around the house until it was time to get ready. Because he had arrived a few minutes early last time, she made sure she was prepared with plenty of time to spare.

At five minutes after the agreed upon time of six, he still had not arrived. Time continued to pass with no Tim or even a phone call to explain his absence. She began to worry. She wondered if she had somehow gotten the wrong day or time, when a full hour passed without Tim showing up or calling.

ON THE GO

Out of worry more than disappointment of a no show, Beca reluctantly retrieved the phone number Tim had given her after their first date and dialed the number. His answering machine kicked in after four rings, so she assumed he must be on the way, but she still left a short message. Hunger pains were causing her discomfort, so she nibbled on a few cookies while still anticipating his arrival.

Eventually she prepared herself a quick meal, when it became apparent he wasn't going to show up that evening. Hoping for a phone call yet to ease her anxieties, she stayed up later than she normally would, but it never came.

Exhaustion eventually took its toll, forcing her to retreat to the bedroom. When a couple more days passed without any explanation or even a phone call, Beca made a mental note to write Tim off as a lost cause. It greatly disturbed her, because she had considered him someone she really liked and wanted to get to know better.

Sunday afternoon she had just dozed off in the living room chair when the phone rang. By the time she realized what it was and had gotten up, it had already been picked up by the answering machine.

The male speaking identified himself as Sal Bingly, then asked her to call him as soon as possible. She quickly picked up the receiver hoping to immediately catch Sal. Fortunately he was still on the line and once again identified himself and inquired if he was talking to Beca Stone.

Before the conversation even had a chance to continue, she knew this was not good news. Sal regretfully informed her that Tim had an accident and passed away Friday evening. "I thought I should call you," he stated. I know Tim took you out at least once, and the family told me about the message you left on his answering machine. I'm sorry Beca," he consoled. "I know he really liked you."

The message left her stunned, but she was thankful she knew what had happened.

Two weeks passed without incident, which was almost a welcome change in Beca's life. The wrist had healed well, allowing her to resume normal activities, which included keeping the yard well groomed. She had even taken a couple of short bike rides since her mishap.

One of them just happened to go past the Frosty Dip in town, so she rewarded herself with a superman ice cream cone, on that warm evening. The other had been more into the country, with smells and views of nature that sidewalks and manicured lawns kept at bay. She actually enjoyed both types of ride; each had its place in giving her life variety and relaxation. Maybe that's why she enjoyed riding her bike as much as she did.

A sudden knock on the door startled Beca as she was finishing the evening dishes. Missy had been playfully getting under her feet, and when she jumped slightly, she stepped on Missy's foot, causing an additional burst of adrenaline as her cat squealed in pain. Quickly making her way to the door with her heart doing overtime, she wondered who it could be now.

Opening the door, she came face to face with Jason Crane. She stuttered slightly, "Ah…hi, Jason. This is a surprise." Then she stepped outside, not really sure if she wanted to invite him in. She had not heard from him in a few weeks and was beginning to think he wasn't really interested, but now he was standing at her door. Her thoughts raced ahead of any conversation asking questions like, *why didn't he call first? Is he here just to see me? Is there an issue about the accident similar to the spare tire with Peter?*

The air hung heavy as Jason hesitantly spoke, "I'm sorry if I surprised you, but I have thought about you a lot since we met for breakfast. I had your address from the accident and thought I'd take a ride to see where you lived. When I drove past I suddenly had the urge to see and speak with you. I hope I'm not being to forward by showing up at your door unannounced."

She could tell he was nervous as he spoke quickly and was blushing slightly, but she was somewhat on the defensive having been caught off guard by the surprise visit.

She needed to think quickly and clearly, but her thoughts were in chaos at the moment. She felt upset Jason had shown up unannounced but excited to hear she was on his mind, after all he did take a ride to find out where she lived. Jason grew even more nervous when Beca did not answer him immediately. He started thinking, *I've really blown any chance I had with her. I wish I had not stopped. I should have called. I probably look like a jerk.*

She was driving him absolutely crazy. He was admiring not just her looks but also the fact that she seemed to be in control. Finally bringing the tenseness to a conclusion, Beca answered Jason by admitting he had definitely surprised her.

"It's okay," she commented, bringing some relief to him, but she still left him hanging as to where the conversation was going.

Jason took the lead with renewed boldness, mentioning that when they parted at the restaurant, she had said maybe they could see each other again. Then he asked bluntly, "Can we spend an evening together in the near future?"

Beca being slightly spontaneous, and with her thoughts finally coming together, suggested they talk about it over ice cream right now. "Frosty Dip is just a few miles from here," she stated.

Now Jason was the one surprised, saying that would be great but then hung his head and apologized, humbly admitting he was unprepared and did not have any money with him.

"Well," she said, "I was the one who suggested it, so it would only be fair if I treated you. If you wait out here a couple of minutes I will be right with you."

Jason readily agreed then retreated to his car to wait.

Before leaving her house, Jason pointed to the front of his car saying, I didn't get a chance when we had breakfast to show you how my car looked after they fixed it.

Beca looked at it briefly not really caring but out of common courtesy said while getting in, "It looks different than the last time I saw it."

At the breakfast they had shared, neither one had over indulged in personal information. Now over ice cream they found out they had similar jobs. Jason explained he worked at an auto supply store dealing with both wholesale and retail. She explained the duties of her job to him at the plumbing supply store, which was only wholesale.

He lived in a duplex, liked to read, and admitted to being a couch potato. "Maybe someday," he mused, "I can be on one of those television shows that require all the useless information I've accumulated throughout my years of reading."

Jason dropped Beca off at home, and as they parted with just a handshake, he casually mentioned he would give her a call in the near future.

Back in the house Beca's answering machine was once again blinking, indicating another message. The message was from Rhonda, asking her how life was going and stating it was time for friends to catch up on their lives again, so please call back. It was nice to know her friends cared about her, but sometimes they seemed nosy, although lately they knew very little of her personal life, and she liked it that way for the time being. She decided it was getting late so she would call back sometime tomorrow.

The birds were already singing the next morning as Beca was slowly opening her eyes, trying to clear her mind. "Good, it's Saturday," she said to Missy, who was lying beside her on the bed. The agenda today was to do yard work if the weather cooperated. It was overcast but dry, so Beca thought she should get started on the lawn right away, before the weather changed; after all it was Michigan.

When she came into the house a couple of hours later for a break, she returned Rhonda's call from the night before. They chatted briefly with Beca agreeing to come over for Sunday dinner, allowing the two friends a couple hours together.

By mid afternoon the sun was out, and it grew muggy. She was glad she had the yard work done, including the weeding and the watering of her flower gardens. It was too hot for a bike ride, and the work she had scheduled for today was done, but she had time on her hands, so she decided to go shopping. She really didn't need anything but cherished the idea of an air-conditioned store. She took an early shower and ventured out heading nowhere in particular.

Once on the road, Beca decided she would just take a drive, and then if she felt like shopping later or if she saw something interesting, she might stop. The air conditioner on the car was working hard with the humidity high and the sun bearing down, but Beca was quite comfortable and enjoyed exploring areas previously unknown to her. The car still seemed new to her, and she really enjoyed driving it as she placed a CD in the player and started to sing along.

Hunger pains reminded her the afternoon was slipping by, so she found a fast food restaurant and decided to go inside to enjoy the meal with a table, rather than making a mess in her clean car. Halfway through her meal someone said, "I thought that car in the parking lot looked familiar."

Turning around to see who spoke, she quickly recognized Peter Bell and his daughter, Ruth; they were just sitting down at the table behind her.

He smiled at her before asking if she was happy with the car. She responded that it was the perfect fit. She felt awkward the rest of her meal, knowing Peter was behind her. She hadn't even realized until that moment Peter lived just a few blocks from where she was eating. Finishing her meal, she waved and said in passing, "Enjoy your meal."

She made a hasty exit, thinking, *I have totally embarrassed myself.*

Sunday morning, Beca stayed home from church because she wanted to do some research on the computer. She still had a week and a half of vacation time to use before the end of the year, and suddenly it became a priority to decide when and where she wanted to go.

Last year she had rented a cabin on Hamlin Lake, near Ludington, staying in Michigan. It had been relaxing as she read, sitting by the lake, even dozing off a few times. Her parents had come up for a day; the three of them took the boat provided with the cabin for a cruise on the lake. A couple of those days she had done some cycling, one time leaving early in the morning to go exploring in the town of Ludington. She found it quaint, interesting, and larger than she had contemplated and thus did not get back to the cabin until early evening. Another day she pedaled to the state park and enjoyed a couple of hours hiking on their many nature trails.

This year Beca thought she would like to travel some, especially with her new car, but where could she go alone? After several possibilities, she decided to visit the Wisconsin Dells. She had always heard they were worth the trip, and the area had many other attractions to see and activities to keep anybody from being bored.

She made reservations for the second week in August at one of the hotels, then collected information on several of the other shows and attractions. She figured her boss would not have a problem with her taking the week in August, which was still four weeks away, which was usually a slow period during the year for their industry.

The time had slipped away quickly, and Beca remembered she had promised to go to Rhonda's for lunch. When she drove into the driveway, Roger and Graham came out to meet her. They still had not seen her new ride, and the guys had to check it out. She was happy to show it to them as she expressed how much she liked the stereo system. Twelve-year-old Graham asked if she would allow him to check it out. She said "sure" and turned the key so the system would work before popping the hood for

Roger to check out the man stuff. Rhonda was calling from the house that dinner was ready, so the three headed into the house together for lunch.

After the dinner dishes were placed in the dishwasher, Rhonda and Beca retreated to the backyard patio. Sitting by the table under the umbrella on the warm Sunday afternoon, the two friends started talking. Rhonda was not going to waste any time, and asked Beca point blank if there were any activities in her personal life she needed to catch up on.

Somehow she knew the subject would come up, but she still tried to sidestep it. "I just made plans this morning for my summer vacation," she stated and then elaborated about going to the Wisconsin Dells. She continued by asking Rhonda if her family had ever gone there and wondered if she knew about the numerous campgrounds in the area. Without really waiting for a response, Beca suggested Rhonda's kids were at the age where they would just love it, especially the water parks.

The sidestepping had worked for the moment; Rhonda expressed interest in the Dells, saying that they had never been there. However, this year they had promised the kids a trip to Cedar Point in Ohio, then would try to hit a big city zoo or museum on the way back. They planned to go in just a couple of weeks. "Maybe some other summer in the near future it would work," stated Beca. "I'll go this year and let you know if it's worthwhile."

Rhonda was wise to the ways of her friend. She knew Beca was not telling her everything; she had been too quick reacting to the question, even avoiding eye contact. So, she looked directly at her this time, giving no room to misunderstand the question, once again asking her if she had any new guys in her life that she might want to discuss with her best friend.

Beca had rehearsed this scenario in her mind several times but suddenly drew a blank. Blinking nervously, she stuttered,

"Well, I ah…guess I can't ah…hide everything all the time, now can I?" Then she shyly admitted having breakfast with Jason, the guy who had totaled her car.

She didn't mention the ice cream night or indicate that there may be any real interest. She even tried to smooth it over by saying, "I guess I just wanted to thank Jason for forcing me into buying a new car; it brought a positive change in my otherwise boring life."

Rhonda smiled and would not give up. This time she just looked out over the yard and asked, "What about the guy you bought the car from?"

Before Beca had a chance to reply, Rhonda said, "I saw your eyes light up when we went to pick the car up, and it wasn't just the car that excited you!"

A FRIEND'S ADVICE

Beca had a straight answer to her friend Rhonda's direct question. "Peter is too young for me. Nothing there, sorry to disappoint you."

Once more Rhonda prodded her friend for personal information. "Any other guys you care to discuss, like Tim?"

The words felt to Beca like she had been sucker punched. She had forgotten Rhonda met with the three men in the campground, where she had given Tim her phone number.

Tears came to her eyes as she first confessed actually having had a date with him, before telling Rhonda what had transpired just a few weeks ago. Rhonda immediately apologized to her friend, stating how devastating it must have been for her when she learned of Tim's death.

Beca elaborated by telling her she hadn't told anybody about Tim, not even her own mother. "Jillian knows about him too," confessed Rhonda. "I told her, so I should be the one to let her know what happened. I'm so sorry Beca. I was only trying to help. Sometimes things just happen that we don't understand. Things will work out, I know they will."

With emotions now on edge, Beca excused herself and headed home.

On Monday morning her boss agreed that taking the second week in August for vacation would be a good time. She was thankful he had agreed because she had already made the hotel reservations, but then she wouldn't have done it if she thought it might be an issue. Over the next week Beca was mentally setting her schedule of events in anticipation for the upcoming trip. Looking forward to something always seemed to boost her spirit.

Late in the week she made a mental note on her way home from work to call her brother, Jake. She thought she should visit him before she took her vacation. It was good to stay in touch with her brother and his family as much as possible. They had a good relationship growing up, and now with the hour-plus drive, it took extra effort to see each other.

She called her brother from home, making arrangements to visit him and his family on Saturday. "I want to arrive in time for breakfast," she informed him. "That way I can be back home by mid afternoon."

He asked if she could be there by eight in the morning, reminding her that the boys usually got up early and liked to eat as soon as possible.

"I can do that," she replied, then asked Jake if he would make her his special scrambled eggs.

He laughed as he agreed to make them just for her.

On Saturday, Beca woke to the alarm she had preset. With the hour-plus drive ahead, she did not want to be late for breakfast at Jake's house. Backing the car from the garage, she realized it was raining lightly, the sun was just coming up, and the sky had a yellow-orange hue to it.

I sure know how to pick them, she thought to herself, *today would have been a bad day for outside activities*. She was grateful the overcast sky was blocking the bright sun as she headed southeast toward her brother's house. With the cruise control set, she slipped a CD in the stereo to keep her entertained during the drive.

Arriving ten minutes after the eight o'clock agreement, she knocked at the door and was quickly let in by Jake. "I guess the rain slowed you down a little," he mused, then informed her the scrambled eggs were ready, so she better get to the table before they got cold.

Her three nephews—Carl, Brad, and Robert—were already halfway through their breakfast as Beca, Kris, and Jake took their seats.

In short order the boys finished their breakfast and went to play. Beca excitedly explained her plans for vacation in a few weeks. Kris gave the update on the pregnancy and the boys' activities, mentioning how thankful she was that Carl would be in first grade and going to school all day in the fall, and adding how Brad—who was turning six next month—was starting kindergarten. She continued to elaborate that between the pregnancy and three young boys she needed and deserved a break. Then, looking toward Jake, she gave him credit for being a helpful husband and father.

Jake asked how the eggs were as Beca was finishing hers off.

"Nobody makes 'em like you do," she replied, then added it was worth the long drive. After breakfast Beca found her nephews and read them a few stories, holding their attention for almost twenty minutes, allowing Jake and Kris to share in the breakfast clean up.

"Looks like the rain will continue most of the day," Jake stated. He suggested if Kris was up to it, that they all go to the mall.

Kris replied, "It would make me very happy if the five of you went and let me have a few hours of peace and quiet."

Jake looked at Beca and asked, "Do you think you can handle it with three energetic boys?"

"Well," she answered, "let's see who wears whom out first."

They left Kris home alone as they loaded into the minivan and headed for the mall.

Jake and Beca didn't have much time to really talk because the boys demanded constant attention. It wasn't an issue with either one of them; they were just enjoying time together.

After walking through a few stores, they allowed the boys to spend some time on the playground in the mall, hoping they might burn off some of the extra energy. The mall was busy for being mid July, but that was probably due to the rainy day. After more walking and getting sick of hearing "can we get this or that," the two adults decided to head back home. On the way home, Robert, the youngest, fell asleep almost as soon as they left the mall parking lot.

Back home Kris thanked them for the few hours of peace, while they prepared sandwiches for lunch. She commented, "It sure is easier to accomplish something without wondering what the boys are doing or getting into."

Lunch was ending, and Beca had noticed how well the boys had eaten, so she put Jake and Kris on the spot when she asked, "Is it time for ice cream now?"

Kris sighed. To the boys delight and without saying anything, she went to the freezer and got out the ice cream. Beca stayed for an hour after lunch before saying her goodbyes, then headed home.

By the time she arrived home in mid afternoon—just like she had planned, the rain had ceased, and the sun was making an appearance for the first time that day. Everything was wet from the rain so there were still to be no outside activities, at least not for a few hours. So she decided that she would indulge in something she had wanted to do for some time but had kept putting off. "It's time to rearrange the living room furniture," she said to Missy. Beca thought to herself, *This will give me some exercise along with a new refreshing look, and I will actually accomplish something today.*

A couple hours later, she had rearranged, dusted, and swept the living room. It was a welcome change, but now she thought it could use a few new decorations, maybe a lamp, picture, or some other knick-knack. Again she spoke to Missy who had made herself scarce during Beca's afternoon activities. "I think I'll head out to see what I can find to spruce the living room up, you know, give it a little burst of energy, but first I think we both know I need a shower."

In the shower hunger pains reminded her it was later than she realized, but with shopping on her mind she decided to catch a bite while out.

When she returned home, she was excited with her purchases and proceeded to put them in the places she had pictured in her mind while buying them, she then stood back looking at her work with a sense of pride, it had been a good day.

Sunday morning Beca was at church a little earlier than usual because she wanted to catch up with some of her friends after skipping church last week. When she walked in the door her mother spotted her and came right over. "Well, you do exist," her mom stated. She then asked, "Should we be concerned about you as accident-prone as you seem to be lately? Dad and I still worry about you."

She assured her mother everything was fine and she had just been busy lately, informing her of yesterday's visit to see Jake and his family. She also gave her mother an overview of her vacation plans coming up in a few weeks.

Beca didn't have time to talk to any friends before the service, it seemed her mother had monopolized the time, so they would have to wait until later. After the service it seemed everybody was in a hurry to go somewhere, and the only friend left was Lisa. She told Lisa they needed to have a good talk soon, there had been so many changes in her life, and she really needed someone to confide in. Lisa said "Why wait?" and suggested getting together that evening, just the two of them, stating, "I'm sure my husband can handle the kids for a couple of hours alone." So they made arrangements to meet at a local fast food restaurant at six that evening.

Later that evening in the restaurant, Beca updated Lisa on her ever-changing life. She knew Lisa would not give advice unless asked, and that all her secret revelations were safe. She told Lisa the truth, even including some of her thoughts and emotions. She let her know she had been avoiding her other friend's questions by telling half-truths and leaving out most of the story. She stated, "I just don't want others getting excited for no reason or giving me those 'your not a spring chicken anymore' speeches. Besides," she blurted out, "I don't know if I want my life to change, I'm beginning to like it the way it is."

Lisa sat back with a slight smile on her face, while letting all the information sink in. Beca did not give Lisa a chance to respond as she added, "I needed to talk just to let my emotions out. I'm not even sure what I'm looking for from you, maybe just a listening ear or to talk me through unfamiliar territory. I know you are the one friend who will give blunt and yet caring advice." Beca stopped speaking abruptly and apologized for rambling on, admitting she was confused with what she wanted lately then relaxed slightly and said, "I'm done talking now; your turn."

Lisa answered, slowly saying, "I love you as only a good friend could, and I am a good listener, so anytime you want or need to talk, you know I'll be there for you. But I think it's best if you work through this alone, maybe time and changing situations will help you make decisions along the way." She then demanded, "Follow your heart not your emotions. I know that sounds trite, but that is the best advice I can give. Your heart will tell you what its true desires are—you will know when things are right. Take it slow. I know sometimes you think life is passing you by, but it's not. Be patient in making long-term decisions.

Lisa finished by saying, "I probably said more than I should have, pertaining to that subject. Now let's talk about something else."

So, they talked about upcoming vacations and family. The food had been gone long before the two friends finished talking, and soon the conversation dwindled, so they cleaned their table and parted ways.

The next couple of days, Beca thought about the words her friend Lisa had spoken. She thought Lisa was right, sometimes situations just play themselves out, and she need not try to manipulate things toward what she wanted at that moment. It had been a week and a half since Jason and she had ice cream, didn't he promise to call again? Maybe he just wasn't that interested. She once again reminded herself how she didn't want Mister Pushy.

Thursday evening, Beca went for a bike ride, taking advantage of another beautiful summer evening. Headed no place in particular, she ended up going past the local ball fields, spontaneously deciding to watch one of the games for a while. She really didn't get into sports but did occasionally watch a ball game for something to do. She did however enjoy the atmosphere with all the energy that came with it. After watching a couple of innings, she hit the road for a few more miles on her bike, before heading home for the evening.

Beca could hardly believe two weeks had gone by so quickly as she loaded Missy and necessary things for her into the car. Tomorrow was Friday, Beca's last day of work before taking her vacation to the Wisconsin Dells. She was soon on her way to her mother's, who had volunteered to watch Missy for the week. Then her plan was to take care of the yard work yet tonight. Tomorrow night she would do any final packing before heading out Saturday morning.

Friday evening she was almost packed when her friend Jillian, who had her son James with her, stopped by unannounced. "I was in the area," she said, "and thought I'd see if you were home. I also wanted to tell you to have a safe and relaxing vacation. Do you need me to take care of anything while your gone?" she asked.

Before Beca could answer, the phone rang, so she excused herself momentarily.

It was Jason; he had not called for a few weeks, and now she was preparing to go away. She had vacation on her mind when she answered the phone and wondered if Jillian could hear her. After Jason had identified himself and apologized for not calling sooner, Beca bluntly stated, "I'm really busy and can't talk right now you'll have to call me back some other time." Then she abruptly hung up.

VACATION

"Who was that?" Jillian inquired when Beca hung up the phone.

"Just some salesman wanting my money again," she lied, still keeping Jason and any other personal man issues from her friend. "Everything is already taken care of while I'm gone on vacation," she assured Jillian. "But thanks for asking. She then showed Jillian some of the information pertaining to her anticipated week in Wisconsin. Beca hugged both James and Jillian before they left. She promised to bring a gift back for James.

The alarm was not set, this was her time to kick back, and Beca was in no hurry to leave on Saturday. Even with a slow start, she would be at the hotel by early evening. She had thought about taking the car ferry across Lake Michigan to avoid going through Chicago, but she really didn't mind the drive, and the Saturday traffic shouldn't be that bad, she reasoned. She did watch her money carefully and figured it cheaper to drive around the lake.

Overcast skies greeted her as she loaded a few last minute items into her car Saturday morning. She made one last call to her mom to say good-bye and make sure Missy was okay before leaving. During the conversation her mother made Beca promise to call when she arrived at the hotel, saying, "You know we care about you." But she knew that meant worry, so she promised.

The ride was enjoyable, with very little traffic for the first few hours as Beca sang along with her CD player. Light rain had started, and traffic picked up some when she came into the Chicago area. She had Map Quested the trip ahead of time, deciding to go right up through Chicago, by using the toll roads, she figured it to be the shortest travel distance to the Dells area.

The planned route gave her all expressways except for about fifteen miles between her home and the Dells. The rain had been intermittent the whole trip; it was a good day for driving. The car did well on mileage, but the fuel tank was small, so she stopped once at a toll plaza for fuel en route. That gave her a break from driving and allowed her a chance to grab something for lunch.

Arriving sooner than she had expected in mid afternoon, Beca checked into the hotel before making the promised call to her mother. She also left her mother the hotel phone number, before spending an hour relaxing in her room.

Noticing the rain had ceased, with the sun appearing for the first time that day, she decided to take a quick ride around the town to familiarize herself with the area. The ride excited her as she realized just how many different things there were to see and do. Stopping at a restaurant to appease her growling stomach, she grabbed a few pamphlets on area entertainment before sitting down and leafing through them. Later, when she returned to the hotel, Beca admitted to herself it had actually been a long day, so she just kicked back and watched television for the rest of the evening.

Sunday the rain had returned, putting a damper on any outside activities. So she spent the morning collecting information, and then made a list of what things or activities she desired to spend her vacation time on. According to the weather report, the rest of the week would be sunny with the temperature ranging in the eighties.

The kid in her considered squeezing one of the water parks into her schedule. It was a major draw in the area, with plenty of parks to choose from, and with the warm weather it could be refreshing; they also enticed her adventurous side. Sunday afternoon she went to an indoor show, working her activities around the weather.

Beca filled the week with only a couple of different activities each day, as she had allowed herself only a certain amount of money for the week. *Last year's vacation was frugal*, she told herself, *and this year you need to spoil yourself a little*. But she still had limits and diligently stuck to them.

She spent a couple of days venturing to areas beyond the Dells, because she had found things of interest on some pamphlets in the hotel. Midweek Beca called her mother to assure her she was doing well, then reminded her she would come directly to her house on the return trip Sunday to retrieve Missy.

The vacation was one of the best she had ever taken, never hurried but full of activity, and the weather had for the most part cooperated. She was proud of herself for actually having done the water park thing, thoroughly enjoying it one hot afternoon. The boat ride tour of the Dells was absolutely beautiful with the sun highlighting the different formations of rock.

Beca concluded that clocks speed up during vacations. The week had slipped by so rapidly. She checked out after a late breakfast Sunday morning and fueled her car before heading toward home. She decided to follow the same route back home she had come on just a week earlier.

The drive gave her time to reminisce about the week that was coming to a conclusion. It made her smile, and she was grateful for the change of pace from the routines of life. Not really needing to concentrate much on the driving because of light traffic and an easy route, Beca had plenty of time to take snapshots of her life.

Once again she mused how lucky she was to have met another man who was showing interest in her, even if it was by accident. She knew some things about him but didn't really know him. Was he the man for her?

What about the possibility of her friends helping her find another someone special? Like Rhonda had cleverly done during the campout. She never really got a chance to know Tim. Now she could only wonder if things could have worked out with him. She actually enjoyed fantasying her life possibilities, even wondering if the guy who had owned her car was a possibility.

The drive back seemed much shorter than when she had driven out a week earlier. Maybe because she didn't want to return to her normal routine or she had been so deep in pleasurable thought that time didn't exist.

Arriving at her parents' home mid afternoon, she collected Missy and promised to tell her parents all the details some other time because she was tired and she also needed to get home to unpack. Missy must have really missed her because she usually rode in the passenger's seat but on the trip home today she pushed her way onto Beca's lap, making it difficult to drive. Beca had also missed her, so she allowed it, driving with one hand and resting the other on Missy.

Back home she got busy unpacking and catching up with the accumulated mail. She noticed the answering machine was blinking. She decided to take care of other things first; whoever it was could wait.

Speaking out loud to Missy, Beca said, "Coming back from vacation is the hardest part. You anticipate going, and getting ready is fun, but when you return it all needs to be cleaned and put back. Then you get to catch up on all the work around the house that was neglected while you were off relaxing. Catching up from a refreshing and relaxing vacation almost demands another one."

Missy was glad to be home and didn't seem to care or understand as she purred quietly while rubbing against Becas legs.

With the car emptied out and washing machine started, Beca sat down to rest for a few moments after getting something to eat. While collecting her thoughts, she started going through the mail. She found nothing unusual or demanding, so she placed the small pile on the desk to be dealt with later. After everything had been put away or was being washed, Beca headed for the shower—thinking the cleanup had gone well and had even taken less time than she anticipated.

Once out of the shower, Beca again noticed the blinking light on the answering machine. Now she needed to catch up on who had called during her absence last week. The first two messages someone apparently just hung up, then there was one from Rhonda, who stated she just remembered the vacation thing and would call back next week, it was nothing important—just calling to talk.

Beca's face turned pale when she heard the next message which was left by Jason. She suddenly remembered the last phone call they had, just before she went away. He had called at the wrong time—she was busy, and Jillian had been there, so she had told him to call another time. Then she had forgotten about him with all the excitement of vacation.

She surmised Jason had no idea she had gone on vacation for a week, so he probably had called back the next day. Maybe the two hang-ups had been him.... Now what did he think of her? Did she ruin the relationship?

Now I need to call him and explain the situation. She scolded herself for being inconsiderate. She also felt embarrassed for not calling him back before she left. It would have been easier then than it is going to be now. Her mind snapped back to reality when the machine finished. Lost in her thoughts, she had not actually heard the message Jason had left for her.

Hitting the play button again, she listened instead of letting her mind jump to conclusions. "Beca," she heard him say, "sorry I caught you at a bad time Friday. You seem really busy lately, so I hope everything is all right. Please give me a call when you can. My number again is 555-2143." Then he added before hanging up, "If I've offended you in some way, I'm sorry, please let me know if I did because I didn't intentionally do so."

The message had come on Thursday, time enough to cause additional anxieties due to lack of communication.

Beca felt her heart race as she contemplated what to do. She really didn't want to deal with it right now, but thought the longer Jason went without an explanation, the harder it was on him and possibly her too. She knew this would not resolve itself, and now it would bother her until it was dealt with. She made the decision to call Jason and explain to him how her vacation had caused her to create a problem without even realizing it.

Dialing the number, she was so nervous she hit the wrong number and had to hang up and try again. The phone rang one, two, three, then a fourth time before his answering machine finally came on. Was he now playing games with her? Did he have caller ID? Was he home or not? Her mind raced trying to decide whether to hang up or leave a short message, but before she could decide she heard the beep.

COMPLICATIONS

The words just exploded off her tongue as Beca quickly talked to Jason's answering machine. She was reluctantly returning the call he had left her days before. "Jason, this is Beca. I'm sorry for the missed calls. I've been on vacation for the last week. Please call me back, and I'll fill you in. Thanks, bye."

With that she hung up the phone and sighed, thinking, *now it's his turn to decide where this goes; if he's understanding it shouldn't be an issue*. Maybe someday they could laugh about it, but right now she had the sick feeling of disappointing someone.

The rest of the night was quiet and uneventful. Jason did not call back. She even remembered to set the alarm before retiring because tomorrow it was back to work at the usual time.

Monday flew by for her at work as she returned to her daily routine. Throughout the day she shared with her coworkers her vacation adventures. Arriving home she barely got in the house before the phone rang. Beca braced herself, thinking *here it goes*, then she answered with a soft "hello," but it was only Jillian inquiring how the vacation went. She breathed a sigh of relief but actually had wished it were Jason, so she could put her anxieties to rest.

Once Jillian had heard the highlights of Beca's trip, she informed her they were taking James to the Ford museum and possibly the zoo in Detroit at the end of the week. "By the way," Jillian continued, "James wants to speak to his auntie, so here he is."

James got right to the point with Beca, by asking her, "What did you get me, Auntie?"

She was prepared for the question and answered, "It's something special just for you, but I can't tell you 'cause Auntie wants to see your face when she gives it to you. Maybe sometime this week yet I can come to your house and give it to you."

He seemed satisfied with the explanation for the moment.

Summer was passing quickly, although one could not tell, as the mid August days were hot and dry. Beca noticed the only reason her lawn needed mowing was to keep the weeds to a proper length. The grass turned brown as it went dormant, due to a lack of water on the light soil her home sat on. The multiple colors of the gardens brightened her yard and her spirits. The grass would come back when it rained, so she let it run its course, but the flowers would be done for the year if they dried up, so she kept them watered. She always enjoyed the late summer and fall, knowing eventually the frost would end her flower season. But until then her gardens were a priority, so she tended them well.

Beca was pleased with how quickly she finished up on the yard work, because she still needed to go grocery shopping that evening. Taking a walk around the house, she noticed a few areas needed some minor touchup paint. Not wanting to waste a trip later in the week, she decided to swing by the paint store on her way to get groceries; then she would already have the supplies when she found the time.

Tuesday, as Beca was heading home from work, she made a spur of the moment decision to swing by Jillian's house, hoping they were home so she could give James the gift she had bought him while on her vacation. She assumed they were home because both cars were in the garage when she knocked on the door. Chad answered and let Beca in, stating loudly enough for James to hear, "Auntie Beca is here."

James ran right into her as he came running around the corner into the kitchen where she was standing. "Careful, big guy," she warned. Then she held out a bag for him to open.

Curiosity was written all over his face as he quickly opened the bag, saying, "For me?"

Grabbing the item from the bag, James found a shirt, which he quickly dropped on the floor, once again peering into the bag hoping for something else. Beca knew a little boy wanted more than a shirt, so she had gotten him a second gift.

He happily pulled out a toy helicopter while Beca explained that in the Dells area where she took her vacation, they gave rides on helicopters. James was so excited he immediately ran away to play with his new toy, without even saying "thank you."

Chad apologized for his son and thanked her for the shirt and the toy. She headed for the door, saying, "Sorry, I can't stay. I just wanted to take care of my promise before I found it in my car three weeks from now."

Jillian replied, "I'm sure James would remember and remind you."

Upon returning home Beca again found a message on the answering machine. This time it was Jason saying he was not upset but that he understood, asking her to please call him back at her earliest convenience. He concluded by saying it would be nice to actually talk to her instead of a machine.

She made the decision to call after dinner because she was really starving, and Missy needed some attention. She also reasoned the conversation may be long, they had not talked for a week and a half, and so much had happened, but then she asked herself, *How much does he really want to hear?*

She threw a small pizza into the oven, took care of Missy, got the mail, and started a load of laundry. The timer went off, indicating the pizza was done, so Beca sat down to her meal in solitude.

Just as she placed the dirty dishes on the countertop by the sink, the phone rang. She wondered why she had never seen the need in the past to have caller ID. Picking up the phone she heard a male voice, "Hi, is this Beca Stone?"

Beca could not identify the voice but knew it was familiar. Her mind was racing to place it trying not to embarrass herself as he continued, "Do you have a few minutes to talk?"

Still not knowing who it was, she bluntly asked, "Who is this?"

Beca was stunned as the male voice stated, "I'm sorry. This is Peter Bell, remember the guy you bought the car from a few months ago."

Thinking she would never hear from him again after the spare tire issue was resolved, she was bewildered as to the call. Her first thought was that it had something to do with the car again. Returning back to reality from her drifting thoughts, Beca answered his first question replying, "Ah yeah, sure. I got a few minutes. What can I do for you?"

"Well," he began, "I'll get right to the point. I know this might be sudden, but I've had some time to reflect on a few things in my life lately and decided it was time for me to start dating again. To most people it seems rather soon after losing my wife, and I do feel somewhat that way myself. However for some reason I keep thinking about you and finally told myself, at least let her know. Maybe that's as far as it goes, and that's fine, but I can't live with what ifs."

He hesitated as if waiting for a reply, but Beca—taken off guard—was speechless. Her mind was drawing a complete blank. Feeling the awkwardness of the conversation and the deafening silence from the other end of the phone.

Peter asked, "Are you still there?"

She hesitantly replied, "Yes, I'm here." Admitting to the shock of his call while her mind reeled to make sense of what was taking place.

Peter boldly asked her if they could meet and just talk some evening, suggesting maybe in a public place, trying to ease her discomfort. Then abruptly he said, "At least give me a chance to find out if there could be something between us. Please think about it for a day or two." Then he gave her his phone number, asking her to let him know. Thanking her for her time, he softly said, "Good-bye Beca."

She felt a chill, and it wasn't because she was cold. She slowly hung up the phone, and she just sat there for a few minutes thinking about nothing and everything at the same time.

Beca unconsciously leaned down to pick up Missy, who had been rubbing against her legs. Placing the cat on her lap, she gently stroked its fur as she spoke to nobody in an audible voice. "Is this for real? Am I dreaming? Life is getting so complicated." Her thoughts shifted to Jason. She assumed he was probably expecting a call back from her soon, but at this particular moment she knew she was not thinking clearly enough to talk to anybody sensibly. She knew she needed to make the call but just couldn't, maybe later, but not right now.

Any activities Beca had planned for the rest of the evening were overruled by the sudden thought-provoking phone call she had just encountered. She headed to the bathroom for a shower, hoping to clear her head so that she could make decisions based on facts not emotions.

The shower was refreshing, but her mind was still spinning without any real conclusions. Wandering outside after her shower, she went to look at her flower gardens while breathing the dry summer air. For almost a half hour, she looked at the flowers but didn't really see them. After a while her mind finally had cleared, and now she knew what she had to do. Going back in the house, she dialed Jason's phone number and waited for him to answer.

Jason answered on the second ring with "Hi, Beca." His voice gave no indication as to his mood. She replied, "Either you have caller ID or I was the only call you were expecting."

Jason indicated he had the ID, before mentioning it was good to finally talk in person. He also reiterated how sorry he was for jumping to conclusions pertaining to whatever communication issues there had been in the last couple of weeks.

Beca also apologized for her abruptness on the phone just before leaving on vacation, stating that if she had told him she was leaving for a week it might have prevented an emotional roller coaster for both of them.

The call lasted only about three or four minutes with Jason promising to call after a few days, "If you decide to answer this time." He laughed.

Beca mentioned she had plans of catching up for the next few days after having been gone a week. The real reason she had put him off was to allow herself time to think and not make any rash decisions.

As she placed a bag of popcorn in the microwave she spoke to Missy. "What a day this has been. If the phone rings again today, I'm not answering it. I just can't handle any more surprises; maybe I need a vacation."

Missy meowed as if she understood.

Wednesday evening was cooler, and with the work caught up around the house Beca took a much needed bike ride, releasing the frustrations and energy from the two previous days. As she pedaled on the country roads she could smell the fresh cut hay the farmers were putting up for the winter months. Her mind was much clearer as she tried to put her priorities into perspective.

She thought about Peter as she considered allowing him an opportunity per his request to see if anything could be. Maybe she was the one who needed to know if it could be, she reasoned. There was no harm in meeting for an evening. She made up her mind that tomorrow she would give Peter Bell a call and make arrangements to meet him for an evening. Maybe it was out of curiosity or maybe hopeful thinking, but as Peter had mentioned, then there would be no what ifs. Beca was almost giddy as she pedaled vigorously back home with the renewed energy her decision had given her.

Sticking to her plan, Thursday evening Beca called Peter to make arrangements for dinner. After Peter had named a few restaurants from fast food to elegant, he stated, "Beca, whether you consider this a date or not, I'm paying."

"Okay," she answered as she considered the options before continuing with, "Let's go middle of the road and meet at Dave's Family Dining at…say, six. Does Saturday work, or is that too soon?"

Peter immediately agreed the day and time both worked well for him.

The phone rang again before Beca had a chance to take more than a few steps from it. *Did he change his mind already*, she asked herself, jokingly, thinking it was Peter again. She answered, "It's too late to change your mind."

As soon as the words were out of her mouth, she regretted saying them, not knowing how Peter might react. It was not Peter, the caller hesitated upon hearing the unusual greeting, then responded, "I don't know who you think this is, but it's your mother, and I don't believe that message was meant for me, was it?"

Embarrassed, Beca quickly admitted to having just talked to a friend and had assumed it was them, again giving no hint to her mother as to the friend's identity.

Elaine Stone asked her daughter if things were back to normal since returning from her Wisconsin vacation. She then suggested Beca come over Saturday evening for dinner. "We are looking forward to hearing all the vacation details from you. Hopefully we can also see a few pictures. Dad says he will grill you the best burger you've ever tasted."

Remembering the agreement she had just made with Peter—not more than five minutes ago—Beca told her mother she already had plans for Saturday evening but was available for Sunday dinner if that worked. Her mother was slightly disappointed having to change the day but agreed to Sunday, knowing her daughter had a life of her own and she needed to respect it.

Friday work just seemed to drag for Beca; the slow season was lasting longer than normal. Another coworker left at noon, getting an early start on his vacation the following week. There were a few small orders to finish, but like the long, hot lazy summer days, nobody seemed to be in a hurry for them. She told her boss to enjoy the weekend as five o'clock finally came, and she headed home.

Having been bored most of the day, Beca decided tonight after dinner was a good time to do the touchup painting around the exterior of her house. It took longer than she had expected, and the sun was starting to set as she finished. She was not only pleased she had accomplished so much, but was proud of a job well done as she did a final inspection of her work. In the shower she wondered how the last few hours felt so much shorter than the eight hours she had at work that day.

Saturday dawned with the sun shining under the building clouds. Beca slept longer than expected; having not set the alarm, she finally woke to the rumble of thunder. *Well*, she thought as she rolled over again, burying her head back into the pillow, *the rain will help the grass, and I'm glad I got all the painting done last night*. Staying in bed felt great as she listened to the rain that was beginning to fall.

Moving slowly—with no agenda for the day—Beca dressed, ate breakfast, played with Missy, then sat in the living room admiring her reorganizing of the room while slowly sipping a cup of coffee. Her mind drifted back to last week's vacation. She mentally walked back through it, which brought a smile to her face. The coffee cup was soon empty, but the rain showed no sign of stopping. Beca decided to go shopping, maybe even finding something new to wear tonight at the dinner with Peter.

The rain finally let up around noon with the sun trying to poke through the clouds. Beca still wanted to take a bike ride today if possible. Feeling somewhat defeated for not finding any new clothing she liked while shopping, she headed home for lunch. After lunch she puttered around the house for another hour, hoping it would dry up some before taking her bike out. She liked to bike but didn't relish the idea of getting wet, and certainly didn't need a repeat of the last bike ride with rain combination.

Beca did take a short ride before determining everything was going to remain wet for a while, so she returned home to take a shower before curling up in a chair, while burying herself in a book until it was time for dinner with Peter that evening.

INFORMATION OVERLOAD

As the time neared for Beca to meet Peter for their date, she thought to herself, *I really don't know anything about this guy, so maybe it was a good idea meeting in a public place.* She had not confided in anyone about her plans to meet Peter tonight; now she wondered if she should have. To ease her mind she wrote a note, saying where she went and whom she was meeting, and left it on the kitchen countertop, reasoning that if for some unknown reason something happened, the note would be found.

Thinking about the note as she drove to meet Peter, Beca chided herself for being paranoid, but was comforted in the fact nobody else would find the note. She would destroy it as soon as she arrived home.

Beca arrived at Dave's Family Dining a few minutes early. She had been past the restaurant several times but had never eaten there. It was one of the suggestions Peter had given when they were making dinner plans. Once inside the lobby, she quickly spotted Peter, who was motioning for her to come and sit next to him in the waiting area.

"I got here early, so I already put our name in," he stated. "It looks like about a twenty-minute wait."

Beca sat down next to Peter and made the comment, "You can usually tell a good restaurant by the length of wait during the prime dinnertime."

Peter nodded and replied, "I assure you, it's good. I've been here a few times before."

The conversation remained on the surface with each asking how the other's day had been. There were also comments on the rain and hot summer days as they watched other patrons in the waiting area.

"Bell," the hostess called, "your table is ready."

Peter stood up and waited for Beca to precede him as they followed the hostess to their table. They sat down facing each other in the booth they had been directed to, at the far end of the dining area.

As they began looking over their menus, the waitress greeted them with a warm smile and asked if she could get them something to drink. Beca returned the smile and asked for decaf coffee. Peter quickly followed with, "Make that two."

The waitress told them of the nightly specials then returned to the kitchen for their coffees.

Returning with the coffees only a minute later, the waitress asked if they were ready to order, and they both replied "yes."

After the waitress left with the orders, Beca started sipping her coffee. When she glanced up at Peter, she noticed he seemed slightly dazed but was staring at her. This made her rather uncomfortable.

"You are more beautiful than I even remembered," he said as he stirred some sugar in his coffee. "Thank you for agreeing to meet me tonight. Please let me explain myself," he said in a pathetic manner that melted her heart, convincing her to lower her guard a little.

"Okay," she replied, not sure where Peter was going with the conversation. She was glad they were at the far end of the dining area, allowing them some privacy.

He began by saying, "First impressions are the most important when people meet, and I was very impressed the day you came to test drive the car. I stated before that my wife had passed away a couple of months before I first met you. I know it may seem too soon for me to be interested in someone else, but please hear me out before you jump to a conclusion.

"My wife, Linda, was diagnosed with a rare heart disease, almost two years ago. Short of a heart transplant, there was little hope. We had many tests done, tried other doctors and different medicines, but eventually we both knew the day would come, so we prepared the best we could. It was really a long good-bye, but at least we had the opportunity to say good-bye. Some couples never get the chance. Linda made me promise to continue living for her and our daughter, Ruth, whom I believe you met when you picked the car up. Most of my mourning was done even before Linda passed away."

Just then the waitress appeared with the food, halting the intense conversation.

When the waitress left, Peter continued by saying, "I actually hated the feeling that came over me when I first met you, but the last couple of months I kept thinking about you, and I know Linda wanted me to move on as soon as I could. I really don't know if anything between us is possible, but I need to know for sure. I'm sorry for being so forward, but I felt you needed to know my circumstance and my thoughts. I was waiting out of respect for Linda, but lately had a feeling that if I waited too long, opportunity may be passing." Peter concluded, "I'm only asking you to give me a chance to know who you are, Beca Stone."

Peter briefly looked into Beca's eyes and said, "Excuse me." He bowed his head and prayed a silent thank you over his meal, causing her some discomfort. She had attended church most of her life and knew about God, but He had not really been a priority in her life.

Beca had already made a decision to keep the relationship shallow for the moment. Especially right now, while she tried to sort out the information Peter had just given her. When Peter lifted his head after the prayer, she changed the topic by asking where his daughter, Ruth, was tonight. Peter answered that his mother-in-law had come to the house, volunteering to watch Ruth until he returned that evening. "She loves spending time with her granddaughter whenever possible, and she lives nearby, so this works out good for both of us. Our relationship remains strong," he commented.

Realizing he had given Beca a lot to work through in just a few minutes and that he had been doing all the talking, Peter said, "Sorry to monopolize the conversation. Is there anything you want me to know up front?"

With her mouth full at the moment, she held up a finger indicating he give her a moment. After finally swallowing she said, "I'm actually glad you shared about your wife. I did have some reservations pertaining to the issue, but your explanation has answered a few of my questions. You have helped me understand." She continued, "I really know nothing about you. Can you fill me in with the basics like age, job, and hobbies?"

"How old do *you think* I am?" he asked in reply, trying to make a game of her question.

Beca looked intensely at his face before answering. "I'm guessing late twenties, maybe twenty-eight or nine."

Peter smiled before speaking, "People are always thinking I'm younger than I really am. The truth is, I just turned thirty-one about three weeks ago."

Pleasantly surprised, Beca dropped her jaw slightly and exclaimed, "You're kidding. I would not have guessed that." Then she openly admitted she had considered not meeting him, simply because she thought he was much too young for her.

"Too young?" he shot back. "If I'm correct, we are probably the same age."

Beca snickered as she said, "Sorry to disappoint you, but I'm an older woman. I'm already thirty-two and will be thirty-three before the end of the year. My birthday is in December."

Without hesitation Peter replied, "I can live with that. My wife, Linda, was almost a year older than me too, I must have a thing for mature women."

The tenseness wore off after the initial conversation; the two started to relax as they indulged in their meals.

The waitress stopped by to top off the coffees and asked if Peter and Beca needed anything else. They both replied "no thanks." When she left, Beca made comment to Peter that the restaurant was a good choice. "The food was delicious," she stated. Then added, "The portions could have been slightly smaller."

Peter continued with the game he had started, by asking Beca, "So what do you think I do for a living?"

Engaging in the game, she took a long look at Peter and suggested, "You look slightly rugged, so I'm guessing you do some kind of construction."

"Actually," said Peter, "you're not far off. I am a finish carpenter who builds cabinets and does trim work in homes." Then he searched her face before commenting, "My guess is you work indoors at something that keeps you physically fit."

Beca cheerfully responded, "You're partially correct. I work indoors at a wholesale plumbing supply store, but the only exercise I get by my desk is jumping to conclusions, climbing the walls, or running my mouth." She laughed softly. Peter noted her wit and admired her humor.

"Didn't you mention three things you wanted to know about me?" questioned Peter. "I forgot the last one. What was it again?"

"What do you enjoy doing to fill your time?"

"That's an easy one," Peter told her. "My first responsibility is my daughter, Ruth, and that takes most of my time. Beyond that Linda and I enjoyed camping together, which I have not had the opportunity to do lately with things the way they have been. We have a small pop-up camper," he continued, "so hopefully next year Ruth and I can spend a few days enjoying nature together."

Then he turned the question back to Beca by asking, "And what about you?"

She told him she enjoyed being outside, how working in the yard was enjoyable to her. She also indicated her love of biking, "Pedal bike with no motor," she stressed, "that's where I get the workout that keeps me in shape."

Finished with his meal, Peter sat back just listening and admiring Beca, but said nothing.

The waitress returned to refill the coffee cups, asking if they still had room for dessert. Beca said she had enough, but Peter decided to order a piece of apple pie. As they sat momentarily in silence, Beca started to reflect on the evening for the first time. She realized she had let her guard down and was talking to Peter like an old friend. She had not expected that to happen, especially after the initial rough start, but now she felt comfortable. The pie was delivered, and before Peter started to indulge he said, "It really is nice to have an adult conversation."

As Peter finished his pie, he leaned on the table, closing the gap between them. Peering into Beca's eyes, he said, "I know this may sound weird or even forward, but I have really enjoyed our time together tonight, and the time has flown." Then he asked, "Would it be possible that maybe we could walk around the mall together for a little while? The night is still young, and I have the sitter all evening."

Beca liked the idea but remembered she hadn't told anybody about Peter, and if she was seen with him, she knew the questions would fly, and she just didn't want to deal with that right now. Then she shivered as she wondered what if Jason saw them together. How could she put herself in that precarious position?

Peter was still leaning on the table, searching Beca's eyes, waiting for an answer. She knew her answer could send a message, and she certainly didn't want to ruin what could be a possible future relationship. She thoughtfully contemplated her options before answering Peter, who was now getting nervous because Beca was taking her time answering.

Not hinting the real reason for avoiding the mall, Beca, suggested they go to a nearby park. "I told you I like to be outside."

Peter agreed the evening was nice enough to spend outside. He paid the bill like he said he would. They left the restaurant, driving separately to the park just a few miles away.

Peter, who arrived first at the park, walked over to meet Beca as she was getting out of her car. "That car just seems to fit you; I think you look good in it," he commented. "Maybe the car was fate bringing us together."

She let it slide without any further comment, after all this was really their first date. She was not going to let him believe—at least not at this point—there may be any long-term relationship possibilities.

The rest of the evening in the park was spent admiring nature and watching people. As the sun started to set, Beca told Peter she had better be heading home. Before parting, Peter held both of her hands while looking directly into her eyes, then simply stated that he had really enjoyed her company and again thanked her for sharing the evening with him. He boldly asked if there was any possibility of spending more time together in the future.

This time she did not need time to think about her options. She responded almost too quickly, by blurting out, "I would like that very much." She thanked him for dinner and the evening together before getting back in her car to head home.

Once in the car, Beca breathed out a sigh of both satisfaction and happiness. As she pushed a CD into the player she wondered how the date had gone by so quickly. She was pleasantly surprised that she had enjoyed it so much. *Slow down*, she told herself, *you are making too much out of this.* Then she reminded herself of Jason and the relationship that had already started there. She began to wonder if she was getting into a situation she couldn't handle, but she secretly relished the attention and wanted it to continue, at least for a while.

Sunday Beca was at church slightly earlier than usual, hoping to catch her friend Lisa. Lisa was the only friend she had recently shared anything with about men in her life. After a short wait, she spotted Lisa and made a gesture indicating she wanted to talk to her. Just as she told Lisa she had a guy update for her, Beca's mother came over, and the conversation quickly changed to the usual, "it's good to see you today," and comments about the weather. It was soon time to sit down for the service, so Beca mouthed "later" to Lisa, and she nodded in agreement.

Beca hardly heard the sermon because her thoughts were many miles away. After the service, she pulled Lisa into a corner away from everybody else, then whispered to her about having a date last night with the guy she bought the car from. "I had such a good time," she told her friend. "I almost feel guilty. We both know for the most part guys have been absent in my life, now there are two at the same time. And to tell the truth it's both scary and exciting."

Lisa just shook her head saying, "Be careful, Beca. With a game like that you just might end up losing both of them."

"I know," she replied enthusiastically, "but at this point I don't really know either one of them, but I want to. I certainly don't want to throw myself into one relationship wondering if the other might have been the right choice!"

The conversation ended abruptly when Beca's mother sought her out, informing her that dad was starting the burgers as soon as they returned home from church. Lisa smiled as she waved good-bye and turned to leave.

Beca felt frustrated driving to her parents' home. Lisa had not really helped her feel better about the situation or given any solid advice to grasp. The best option right now, she thought, would be to keep everything as quiet as possible, while taking both relationships slowly. She convinced herself she couldn't make wise decisions with limited information.

Josh Stone already had the burgers on the grill when his daughter arrived. With the smell drifting in the wind, Beca took a deep breath while approaching her father next to the grill. "I hope they taste as good as they smell," she said.

Her father replied, "You should know by now that nobody makes a better backyard burger than your dear old dad."

"Well then," she retorted, "there had better be two of them on there for me."

She excused herself to help her mother set the table on the patio.

Before long the two women heard, "I hope you're ready, 'cause here come the most perfectly grilled burgers, done to perfection. Get 'um while they're hot." Then Josh Stone placed the platter of burgers on the patio table.

During the meal, to make small talk, Elaine asked her daughter, "So what's new in your life that you need to catch us up on?"

She was glad her mouth was full of juicy burger, giving her time to ponder a good answer.

When she was able to talk, she told them how she had done some painting around the house and how work had been slow lately. She explained she had done some shopping, and that the rain had interfered with plans to go biking on Saturday. Her parents accepted the updates and did not question her weekly activities any further.

"Those burgers were some of your best dad, but I can't eat another bite," Beca said.

"I guess we can wait for the ice cream dessert I prepared," replied Elaine while she started cleaning up the table.

As Josh took a load of dishes into the house he commented, "I think it feels more comfortable in here than in the hot sun." So he sat down at the kitchen table and asked Beca for her vacation pictures from the Wisconsin Dells.

The pictures she had taken turned out well, but she wasn't in any of them, so her mother asked if she was sure it was her vacation.

Beca smiled at her mom's lame joke and deadpanned back, "Somebody had to take the picture you know." Then she told them how she had done the water park thing, went a couple of days to see areas beyond the Dells, and had even taken in a few shows, including a water ski show.

Her father said it looked and sounded like an interesting place that they had never been to, commenting maybe some day they would go but probably skip the water park.

Later while eating the ice cream dessert, her father mentioned Jake and Kris were coming over for Labor Day, so if she didn't have any plans it would be nice to have the whole family together. "I'll grill another one of my special burgers for you," he added with a twinkle in his eye.

Beca thought briefly as to what plans she had and replied, "That would be great. I'll figure on it."

Arriving home mid afternoon, Beca once again had a message. She assumed it was Jason who had promised to call in a few days, and the few days had passed, so she was expecting his call. To her surprise there were two messages and neither was from Jason. The first was from Rhonda who must have called just after Beca left for church. She just wanted to say good-bye; they were leaving for the week, headed to Cedar Point in Ohio, and whatever activities or entertainment they found along the way. Then she added, "I enjoyed our early summer girls only camping and had a great idea. Why don't we have another in a few weeks? Say mid September, before the weather turns cold. It's just been a while since the three of us have had a good chat. Think about it while I'm gone. Please call Jillian to see what she thinks. Maybe we can make plans when I get back."

The second message was from Jillian stating they were back from their two-day trip to Detroit. She also said she had talked to Rhonda about another camping trip for the three of them this fall; then simply said call me and hung up. That was the last message, now Beca was wondering if Jason had forgotten, or if she had seemed to busy the last time they talked. Maybe now he was overcompensating by trying not to crowd her.

Beca made the call to Jillian, asking how the trip to Detroit went. Jillian responded that things had worked out well. 'We had heard the weather report and figured it was going to rain on Saturday, so we squeezed the outdoor activities in on Friday, and did the indoor ones on Saturday."

Jillian asked excitedly if Rhonda had called her about another girls only camping trip. Beca could tell by Jillian's tone of voice, that she already had her mind made up.

"Yes," she admitted, a little less enthusiastic than Jillian. "She left me a message, as you know sometimes I can be hard to get a hold of."

"Well," Jillian countered with excitement still in her voice, "what do you think?"

Beca responded by saying, "It could be getting cold that time of year, however I do like spending time with my friends, so sign me up. I guess I can dress accordingly" she added.

They agreed to get together to plan the outing as soon as Rhonda returned.

Monday was an average day for Beca with the normal routines of going to work, coming home to Missy, and taking care of a few indoor chores. The yard didn't need as much attention this time of the year, allowing her more free time.

With no issues pressing, she decided she could take the bike ride she had tried to take Saturday. With the wind blowing through her shoulder length brown hair, Beca rode at a steady pace, relishing the feeling of freedom and oneness with her bike—it truly was her stress reliever. She pedaled into town with the predetermined idea of passing by the Frosty Dip to treat herself to some ice cream.

The ride was rejuvenating and seemed to eliminate any boredom the day had brought. Beca also felt the exercise cleared her head, and lately she really seemed to need that. Upon entering the house, she headed straight for the shower after her ride, with the idea of relaxing the remainder of the evening.

It was Thursday evening before Jason called again. On one hand he apologized for not calling sooner, but also indicated he didn't want Beca to feel he was pushy. She smoothed it over by telling him she appreciated the thoughtfulness. She was proud of the way she handled the situation, smugly thinking she really did tell the truth. He didn't need to know everything.

Jason asked if they could spend Labor Day together, but Beca turned him down, saying she had planned to spend it with her parents and brother. "Maybe I could spend it with you at your parents' house," he suggested.

Immediately a red flag came up so she answered quickly, "I'd like to keep it just family." She thought, *He didn't want to be pushy, and I certainly don't want my family to know about any men in my life at this time.*

Jason was slightly taken back by Beca's abruptness, but was not easily swayed. He tried another option by asking, "Well, then could I take you out next Friday evening for dinner, just before Labor Day?"

Beca saw his determination and agreed, asking what type of restaurant she should dress for.

Jason said, "I know a neat place called Dave's Family Dining; it's pretty casual, and I've only been there once, but I thought it was good."

Her mind spun as she remembered the evening she had with Peter less than a week ago at the same place. "I would like something a little more formal, being the holiday weekend," Beca stated boldly, not letting on she had another motive.

Jason suggested a place called The Barn, mentioning how an old barn had been made into a better-than-it-sounds dining experience.

"I think I've been past it a couple of times," Beca stated, "but have never eaten there. Is it on Mills road?"

"Yes," Jason replied. "It may not be all that formal, but it is a step up from Dave's." He then asked if he could pick her up at six the next Friday evening.

"That sounds great. I will be ready and looking forward to it," she assured him, then softly said "good-bye" and hung up.

On her way to church Sunday, Beca was listening to the radio and heard a comment from the disc jockey, that summer was almost over, and there was only one week until the long Labor Day weekend.

"This has been one of the shortest summers I can remember," she said back to the radio, reminiscing how busy and exciting the summer had been for her. Still talking out loud, she continued, "I can't believe how much my life has changed because of an accident." She thought of the new car and a couple of guys that were showing interest in her. She smiled before starting to sing with the radio.

At church it was Lisa who sought out Beca this time, motioning her over to a secluded area before asking, is there anything interesting I need to know? She stood there waiting for a reply with piercing eyes. Beca lied, keeping some secrets even from her friend Lisa, by shrugging slightly and responding nothing, "I've just been really busy lately."

Lisa tilted her head slightly with that "I don't know if I believe you" look and asked, "really?"

Beca didn't feel like revealing anything about her personal life at this time, so she changed the subject by telling Lisa how she had enjoyed a couple of bike rides during the last week. Lisa somehow knew Beca was purposefully avoiding disclosing information. She did not fully understand her friend's mood or clam up attitude but did not press the issue, thinking in due time it would all come out.

HOLIDAY WEEKEND

After Beca finished lunch Sunday, she curled up on her favorite chair in the living room with Missy on her lap, and started reading. Suddenly the ringing phone jolted her awake, causing her to jump. Missy who also had been sleeping went flying with a loud "meow." Half dazed from being wakened so abruptly, she answered with a weak "hello." Rhonda on the other end asked—already knowing the answer—"Did I wake you?"

Beca recognizing Rhonda's voice as she slowly woke up answered, "Yes, I guess I dozed off while reading."

Rhonda was excited as she indicated having already spoken to Jillian about camping in a couple of weeks. "You know just the three of us," she reminded Beca.

While Beca was still trying to wake up, Rhonda continued, "Jillian said you were in, so we figured with next week being the holiday, maybe we could go the weekend after. Is that too soon for you?" she asked. Not waiting for an answer Rhonda added, "We don't want to wait too long or the weather could work against our having a good time."

Beca stated she did not have any plans for that weekend, and believed that sooner was a wise move this time of year. After working out the details of who was responsible for what supplies, Rhonda stated that her and Jillian had liked the campground the three went to last time, so they planned on going there again. When all was agreed to, Rhonda told Beca, "If I don't call before the campout, just be at my house as soon as you can after work that Friday night. We'll save time by grabbing some fast food on the way there."

The week was dragging, so Beca really looked forward to the upcoming holiday weekend for a welcomed change of pace. The week started out extremely hot and dry, with temperatures in the nineties and predictions of mid seventies and rain possible for the weekend. *That figures,* Beca thought, *when people want to spend time outside with friends and family the weather doesn't cooperate, but then the weather people only took educated guesses and were wrong quite often.*

Friday the mood at the plumbing supply store was upbeat as everybody anticipated the long weekend. The business activity appeared to be picking up after the slow period they had over the last month, which helped keep some of the boredom away. Beca's coworkers asked if she had plans for the weekend. She gave them only enough information to satisfy their curiosity. She simply told them she was spending time with friends and family, which she justified as truth. They had no reason to believe anything different than what she told them. At five o'clock, they all left, wishing each other a safe and fun holiday.

With a whole hour before Jason was to pick her up, Beca did not feel rushed as she drove home that Friday evening. The weather was overcast, threatening rain as she pulled into the garage at home. She took a shower and was dressed with fifteen minutes to fill before Jason was to be there. So she went through her mail and took care of some bills to fill the gap in time.

Jason was getting out of the car as she came out the door, but he got right back in when he saw her. "I guess you saw me coming," he commented as she slipped into his car. "I was actually coming to the door to escort you, but you didn't allow me the opportunity," he stated. She smiled when he commented, "Just so you know up front, this time I brought money with me, unlike the last time when we went to the Frosty Dip."

She continued smiling as she replied, "I remember, but I also recollect you didn't expect to spend time with me that night when you took a drive to find where I lived."

Jason felt comfortable with Beca as he complimented her by saying, "You look great; maybe I should have dressed better, motioning to his light green polo shirt and blue jeans. He was admiring her shoulder length brown hair, which blended well with the dark pantsuit and burgundy button down shirt she had on.

"You look fine," Beca replied, but made a mental note of his well-worn tennis shoes. They didn't fit the rest of the outfit, but she said nothing, thinking to herself, *he may need a little help in the fashion department.*

At the restaurant, Beca got out of the car while Jason was coming around the backside of the vehicle. He reprimanded her by saying, "I can only open the door for you if you allow me to."

"I'm sorry," she said. "I guess I've been independent so long, it just comes natural doing things for myself." Then she scolded herself for not picking up on the signal he had given at her house about coming to the door for her. He was trying to be a gentleman, but she was not giving him a chance. Walking in front, Beca came to the restaurant door and stepped graciously aside, allowing Jason to open the door for her, which he did without hesitation. She said a soft "thank you" as they ventured inside.

The atmosphere in The Barn was just like its name, it was an old barn someone had made into a classy restaurant. Some of the wall decorations were well-used farm tools, the floorboards were wood, and the lighting had the look of old lanterns. As they signed in, the hostess asked them if they wanted the formal upstairs seating, or the cafeteria style they served in the lower level. Jason said, "I forgot you had the cafeteria style, but I believe we desire the formal this evening." He looked briefly at Beca for approval.

She smiled and nodded her head in approval as the hostess stated it could be a few minutes.

Sitting in the waiting area, both took a gander at the spacious area above them. When renovating for the restaurant, they had left some of the loft above what was now the kitchen, with the dining area open all the way up to the rafters. Above the kitchen were a few larger farm implements for display, completing the atmosphere. As Beca and Jason were admiring the nostalgia the barn displayed, they heard, "Crane for two," and followed the hostess to their table.

Once seated both decided to look over the menu so they could order as soon as possible, not because they were in a hurry, but the restaurant seemed busy, and they were getting hungry. The waitress brought water and asked if she could get them anything else to drink.

Beca stated they were ready to place the entire order. The first thing she ordered was chocolate milk. Beca finished her order, and Jason ordered regular milk, commenting that it wouldn't be right drinking something other than milk in a barn.

Again admiring the rustic look of the barn-style restaurant, Jason and Beca pointed out different things of interest to each other. "It is unique," she commented.

"And it brings back memories of days gone by," Jason added. "I grew up in the country, but not on the farm. Our neighbor had a barn with a few cows in it when I was growing up. I sometimes helped with a few chores, but that is about the only farming experience I have." With a far away look in his eyes, he added, "They're good memories."

The waitress had already brought out their milk and had returned soon after with the food orders, telling them to enjoy their meal. After she walked away, Jason and Beca laughed quietly, looking at each other. They swapped the plates that the waitress had placed incorrectly. Beca asked Jason why he didn't say anything.

He replied, "She looked so busy, I certainly didn't want to make her night any harder than it already was."

She noted his thoughtfulness.

Beca asked, "Didn't you say you had a sister?"

"Yes," he replied. "Her name is Emily; she is three years older than I am, married but has no children and probably never will. She married in her late twenties and was already established in a career she enjoyed, somehow that became her priority. I never bring the subject up because I want to keep the good relationship we have, and it really isn't any of my business."

She continued with the questions, trying to find more out about Jason. She asked him about the couch potato comment he had made about himself when they had breakfast together.

He replied, "I told you I like to read, and I don't have a lot of friends, so I watch quite a bit of TV. Plus I love to watch movies, especially old westerns. I do own the duplex I'm living in, so that gives me some outside activity, but it's really pretty easy to maintain.

"Enough about me," he concluded. "What about you? This can't be a one-sided information meeting.

Beca shoved another forkful of the roast beef she had ordered into her mouth to buy time. When she was able to talk, she replied, "I think you already know most everything. I live a simple life, you know I work, I bike, I putter in my yard and read, that's about it. Jason eyes were fixed on her lips as she spoke.

When she had finished, he gazed upward to her eyes then said, "Yes, I know all that, but I believe you are a mysterious woman who is much deeper than she is letting on. Maybe I want to know who you are not what you do."

Beca—now slightly nervous—blushed as she wondered what he was looking for. She wanted to be careful with personal information, so she said, "I think you know enough for now. Let's just be friends first."

Jason felt the awkwardness and realized Beca was a strong woman who wasn't going to be pushed, so he quickly backed down by saying, "I agree, friends first."

They were both completing their meals, when Jason suggested maybe they could take in a movie together yet that evening. Beca hadn't even thought ahead of time what might take place after the meal. *It would be a short date if we end it now*, she admitted, then made Jason smile by answering, "I think we can work it into the schedule."

As they entered the driveway to Beca's home following the movie, Jason asked if he could walk her to the door. She hardly had time to say "I guess so" before Jason was exiting the car and almost ran around to her side to open the door for her. As he did, she asked, "A little eager, are we?"

Jason admitted during the short walk to her door that he had really enjoyed the evening with her. She unlocked the door then turned back toward Jason, who quickly leaned toward her giving her a kiss on the cheek. With a look of surprise on her face, she blinked a couple of times and stuttered a quick thank you for the evening.

Jason then turned and went back to his car.

Sunday morning at church her friend Lisa came over to say "hello." She didn't push for personal information, deciding that if Beca wanted to talk she would do so. Beca asked Lisa if she had plans for the holiday and how the family was. Then as she was turning away, she slipped in, "We will have to get together to talk in a couple of weeks."

"Sure," Lisa replied as Beca continued walking away to visit with other people, leaving her friend hanging.

Monday morning was Labor Day and the rumble of thunder woke Beca at 5:00 a.m. "Great," she said out loud. "For once the weather forecaster got it right. Couldn't they be wrong today?" She rolled over and tried to go back to sleep, but finally gave up, after another forty-five minutes of constant thunder.

Making it to the kitchen, she got herself a cup of coffee thinking, *today is a holiday I'm supposed to be sleeping in*. She turned on the television to see some news and maybe catch the weather. She sat down with her coffee and heard the forecaster say that the showers should come to a conclusion in another hour, followed by the mid seventies for the day's high. Still in her pajamas, Beca finished her coffee, turned off the TV, and before long dozed off in the chair.

Missy jumped on her lap, waking her up. Briefly confused as to why she was in the chair in her pajamas, Beca's thoughts slowly came together as she remembered the thunder, rain, and holiday all at once. The clock was right at 9:00 a.m. as she went to get dressed and get herself some breakfast. She glanced out the window to check on the rain, which appeared to be done, but everything was still very wet.

Arriving at her parents' house around eleven, Beca noticed her brother's car was already there. Her three nephews greeted her before she had a chance to close the door, while her sister-in-law, Kris, told the boys to give their aunt a chance to get in. She casually informed Beca they had just gotten there and she was the recipient of the energy they had built up from the long ride.

The sun poked through the clouds occasionally, but the yard was still damp from the morning thunderstorm. Kris told the three boys—Carl, Brad, and Robert—to stay in the house. She knew if they went outside they would be covered in something undesirable, and she had not brought extra clothes. The adults sat on the backyard patio, trying to catch up on the latest family information.

Kris told everybody the pregnancy was going well. She was now feeling better than she had the first few months, although she stated the boys do try my patience and wear me out. The guys talked of their jobs and the economy, while the girls talked about kids, shopping, and the latest recipes.

In the course of conversation, Beca mentioned she had gone to The Barn for dinner Friday evening.

"I know where that is," her father said, looking at his wife." "It's on Mills road; it's an old barn made into a restaurant. We have always wanted to try it but have just never made the effort."

Elaine turned toward her daughter and asked, "Is it any good? Should dad and I try it sometime?"

Beca responded, "We really liked the atmosphere, and the food was good. The price seemed fair, so I would recommend it. They also have a choice for type of dining with formal upstairs and a cafeteria style downstairs. It must be good, they seemed pretty busy when we were there."

Jake, Beca's brother looked at her with a quizzical look and asked bluntly, "Did you say *we?*"

She felt really warm as she realized she had slipped, and her brother had picked up on it. Trying to finagle her way out of the situation she answered, "Yeah, I went with a friend. We thought we'd start the holiday weekend off trying something different."

Jake pushed Beca for more information by asking, "So who was the friend? Your not trying to hide anything from your family, are you, Beca?" He lowered his head slightly, but kept looking directly at her.

She turned from his gaze as she responded, "I will keep you informed of my personal life on a need-to-know basis, and right now you do not need to know, little brother."

Beca's father, Josh, jumped in to keep the peace by suggesting he and Jake get the grill started because his stomach was telling him it was time. Jake sensed he had pushed Beca where she didn't want to go, so answered his father by replying, "That's a great idea. I'm sure the boys will be asking for food soon."

Elaine asked the girls if they could help her get the dishes out and prepare the other food; they readily agreed.

No more was said pertaining to Beca's evening or who the mystery person may have been. She did tell her family about the upcoming weekend campout with the girls, admitting she was actually looking forward to it, even if it was rustic and might be cold. Then she reminisced about the previous campout they had in June.

BACK TO NATURE

With the shortened workweek due to the holiday, the plumbing supply store where Beca worked was busy as people returned to their normal work routines. Between work and getting ready for the girls only campout, plus keeping up on things around the house, Beca found no extra time for bike riding during the week like she had hoped.

Friday came quickly, and her excitement about the campout made the workday seem long. The weather looked promising for the next couple of days with no rain and predictions of daytime temperatures in the seventies.

After work Beca stopped home to finish packing the perishables, grabbed a quick shower, and then took care of Missy by putting extra food and water out before she left. When she arrived at Rhonda's, Jillian was already there, so they quickly transferred Beca's gear into Rhonda's vehicle before heading out in anticipation of a fun-filled weekend together.

The three friends talked excitedly as they drove to the same rustic campground they had been at almost three months earlier. Rhonda asked if they could get the same spot.

Jillian answered, "Sure we can. Only crazy people go rustic camping after Labor Day."

After swinging through the drive up at a fast food restaurant, they continued on toward the campground.

Arriving to find their previous spot still vacant, they claimed it quickly, especially when they saw another vehicle entering the campground behind them. Once stopped, Rhonda took command saying, "I suggest we eat our dinners now because cold grease doesn't taste good."

Jillian and Beca agreed, laughing.

In less than ten minutes, the three had finished eating and again Rhonda pushed the agenda saying, "We need to collect firewood first because the sun sets sooner this time of year."

So they ventured in different directions around the campsite to collect the firewood for the evening's warmth and entertainment.

Finally, set up was done, and this time they made sure any food was put in the vehicle for the evening to prevent the raccoons from helping themselves to a treat during the night. The friends sat around the fire as the temperature dropped dramatically with the setting sun. Rhonda commented that with the cooler temperatures they need not worry about bugs, and Beca added in a matter of fact way, "I don't know how any bug could get to us with all the layers we have on."

Rhonda jabbed back at her, asking, "Are you getting soft on me, Beca?"

Just then Jillian gave a big shiver and said, "We either need to have a bigger fire, or I'm going to hit the sack where it's warm."

This time it was Beca being bold as she looked at Jillian and said, "It's way to early for bed. Let's go for the big fire and toast marshmallows; I'm way too wound up to call it a night."

With the fire now throwing flames well above their heads, the friends felt the heat and even backed up a bit. While roasting the marshmallows, each took a turn sharing the experience of their vacation taken during the last month. Rhonda—again being forward as she was at times—asked Beca if her vacations would be better if she had someone to share them with. Then even suggested maybe someone like the guy you bought your car from.

Rhonda gave her that, "well what have you got to say now" look, while Jillian—quite interested herself as to what her friends response might be—was holding her roasting stick straight up, trying not to burn the mallow while waiting to hear the answer. Beca blew it off as no big deal by stating that it might be nice if someday that happened. She gave no indication as to involvement with any male friends.

The conversation dwindled, as they grew tired from the long day. So the three just sat for a while, letting the fire die down before turning in for the night.

Can't be morning yet, its still dark out, thought Beca as she heard Jillian and Rhonda talking outside the tent. The light was just appearing as she asked in a loud voice, "What time is it?"

Rhonda replied, "We don't know. Morning or daytime, maybe breakfast time. Are you hungry yet?"

Beca emerged from the tent to find it brighter than she had expected. She noticed her friends already had fried the eggs up with the camp stove they brought, and it smelled like they were trying to burn the toast. "All right. I'll get up," Beca said, but she scolded her camping companions. "I thought this was a relaxing weekend. You two don't know how to sleep in or relax."

"We did sleep in," Jillan countered. "And now we need a good breakfast before our hike."

Beca groaned. "I'm going back to sleep."

But her friends overruled her decision with a two against one vote.

After finishing breakfast, Rhonda asked the other two what type of sandwich they wanted for lunch during the hike that day. After putting the lunch together, they cleaned the site up to deter the creatures of the wild from coming in and making a mess. Jillian commented to Beca, "Rhonda always wants to explore something new and likes to keep things exciting, so we are trying a different trail than we had on the previous hike. I hope she has her GPS so we can find our way back."

Rhonda—having overheard the comment—said, "I would never purposely mislead my two best friends, besides you both know you like these hikes, and I know that you know. So step it up, it's time to get going."

The early morning chill required sweatshirts as they started on their days venture. The hiking trail Rhonda had chosen for them followed a winding stream. The leaves had just begun turning colors in the early fall, making for an ever-changing scene of beauty. Beca did enjoy the peacefulness of the woods, and she loved being outside. Besides, hiking with her friends was a great stress relief. The friends did not talk initially, choosing rather to listen to the sounds of nature as they hiked. They had each found a hiking stick back at camp before starting out; now they were prodding along the trail with Rhonda in the lead, and Beca in the rear.

The crisp morning air helped Beca clear her mind; she thought about some of the changes taking place in her life. She began to wonder if it was time to let her friends in on what was going on. She knew they cared for her and would keep any secrets she asked them to. But she also knew why she was keeping information from family and friends; it was because they all wanted to help her by giving advice, and sometimes they jumped to conclusions—frustrating her. She just found it easier to tell them nothing at all.

A fork in the trail forced them to read the map before continuing on. The decision made would also determine how long the hike would last. The temperature was slowly creeping up, and with the exercise, all three decided now was a good time to remove the sweatshirts they had needed when their hike started. The collective decision was to take a trail showing a rope bridge along the way, so they continued along the stream path. After that they could again choose a couple different trails, depending on time and type of adventure they sought on the way back.

They had not even gone one hundred yards up the trail, when suddenly a deer jumped up not far from them and ran deeper into the woods. The friends all jumped in surprise at the unexpected noise in their quiet environment. They all laughed, agreeing one reason they wanted to go hiking was to see wildlife—just not that close. Now that the serenity had been broken, the three started commenting on all the interesting things they saw as they continued toward the rope bridge shown on the map.

Just over a small rise, the three spotted the bridge a short distance ahead. As they approached it Beca said to no one in particular, "I thought this was going to be a small bridge, I don't know about this." She shook her head. All three scanned the scene of the rope bridge stretching almost one hundred feet across and twenty feet above the stream below. It did have boards on the bottom giving it some stability but only had ropes on the sides. Beca asked if it might be safer just going down the embankment and walking through the stream, rather than risking their lives on the bridge.

Rhonda laughed at her and insisted it's safe. "I'll show you," she said as she started across it alone. When she got to the center she motioned for her friends, saying, "Come on, it doesn't sway much. Besides, you don't want to miss the view from here.

Jillian looked at Beca then she gingerly stepped onto the bridge. "It can't be that bad," she insisted. "Come on let's go."

Now all three, were standing in the center of the slightly swaying bridge. Beca admitted it really wasn't that bad. They spent a couple of minutes admiring the different views from the bridge, looking all around and even down into the stream. As they continued to the other side of the bridge, Rhonda told her friends she was glad they chose that trail. The rope bridge was a highlight to be remembered. She even stated that her husband, Roger, might want to come see it with her someday.

Now on the other side of the stream, the trail led them just a few hundred feet then came to another fork. This time there were a couple of benches under a two-sided shelter, with a map of the surrounding trails posted for hikers. Rhonda suggested it was a good place for an early lunch, and they could rest their feet for a little while. Beca mockingly said, "Maybe we'll see other hikers like the last time we ate lunch in the middle of who knows where."

Jillian, looked at her and replied, "I don't think so. Not this time of year. Except for one deer and a few squirrels, we haven't even seen wildlife."

Beca—not missing a beat—followed with, "I think I'm with the wildlife."

Before eating they looked at their hiking options on the map displayed, Jillian suggested a trail that would get them back to camp by early afternoon. Rhonda wanted a longer hike, but Beca cast the deciding vote, agreeing with Jillian's choice.

As they sat eating lunch, Rhonda asked Beca if she had any updates on guy situations she wished to share with her friends.

She just sat there eating her lunch as if she had not heard Rhonda, so Jillian—also curious—jumped in prodding her, "We know you heard the question, and you know we know. I'm just guessing now because usually we get a quick reply but not this time, so what's going on Beca? Do you want to share with your friends?"

As soon as she spoke, Jillian felt she may have pushed her too far and immediately apologized for it saying, "Look we've been friends for a long time, and you know we both care about you—that's all, we just care. Jillian then glanced over at Rhonda who agreed with her before they both went back to eating their lunches.

Beca wiped her mouth after taking a drink. While staring out into the woods, she calmly stated, "There has been someone lately, but I don't know where it's going yet, and I certainly don't want my friends drawing conclusions."

Rhonda and Jillian looked at each other thinking, *the dam has broken maybe she is finally ready to talk.* They had both suspected that she'd been keeping something from them for a while.

"Is it the guy you bought your car from?" asked Rhonda. Without waiting for an answer, she continued, "I remember the way you acted around him when we picked up the car."

"What?" exclaimed Jillian. "I didn't know anything about this. How long has this been going on?"

Beca turned toward her friends and quietly replied, "No, it's the guy that totaled out my car, and we've only had a couple of dates, so don't go ballistic on me."

The two friends fired a few more questions at her, prying for more information, but Beca coldly responded, "Sorry, I'm not at liberty to divulge any other details at this time."

Then she abruptly jumped to her feet and forcibly said, "Let's get going. We came to hike not chitchat."

The other two were astonished at her boldness but didn't argue, quickly getting up to follow Beca down the trail they had previously chosen.

"Who chose this trail?" Rhonda inquired.

The trail wound down into a ravine before becoming almost a straight steep climb up the other side. Jillian shot back at Rhonda who was still taking up the rear. "I would never have guessed you to be the complainer when things got tough."

Defending herself, Rhonda informed Jillian, "I wasn't complaining; it's just that when I pick a trail I try to make it as easy as I can for my friends."

Beca felt the need to add her input, so she stated, "You can't tell what a trail is like by looking at a flat map. And how do you know," she added addressing Rhonda, "we didn't choose this trail to give our friend a challenge?"

"Okay," Rhonda said. "I give up. You got me. Lead on, oh fearless one."

Arriving back at the camp, Jillian said, "I don't know about you guys, but I need to sit and recuperate for a while." She plopped down in one of the chairs next to the fire pit.

Beca said, "Me too." She grabbed a book to read before taking residence in a chair next to Jillian.

Rhonda was not going to spoil the party, so she also sat down and began poking around in the ashes from last night's fire with the walking stick she still had in her hand.

After only fifteen or twenty minutes of sitting in silence, Rhonda got up and informed her two friends she was going to gather more firewood for the evening, and if they wanted to help, they could. Beca answered, "I'm enjoying my book right now."

They both looked over at Jillian and smiled, when they realized she had fallen asleep.

Rhonda had found enough firewood alone, so the other two had gotten out of the task. She really didn't mind the additional romping in the woods. Rhonda had considered the morning hike to be to short. She decided she was not going to waste the afternoon sitting around like her friends intended to do. With plenty of firewood stockpiled, Rhonda started the fire saying, "If we're staying here the rest of the day, we may as well have a fire so it feels like camping."

By this time Jillian had waken from her mid-afternoon snooze, and Beca was tired of reading, so the friends sat by the fire, talking.

"So, Beca," Rhonda injected into the course of the conversation, "is there anything else you want your friends to know about your personal life?" She emphasized the *personal* as she continued, "You have our undivided attention out here in nature. If you don't fill us in now, we may not have the opportunity for some time. You know, just the three of us without distractions."

Beca demanded, "Was this campout a trap? Did you two conspire to gang up on me? I know both of you are good friends and care about me, don't you think I've kept you informed already?"

Jillian spoke softly, trying to keep the conversation at a friendly level. "You're right, Beca. We only ask because we care, and if I remember correctly, during the hike this morning you surprised us. We now know there is someone of interest, but we are not making any assumptions, so help us understand—share with your friends so we can be happy with you."

Silence fell as each one of them stared into the fire wondering who was going to speak first. Was Beca upset with her friends? At that moment both Rhonda and Jillian wished they had not pushed the issue, remembering that she had abruptly stopped the flow of information at the shelter on the trail. A crow called in the distance, a squirrel was playing nearby, and the fire crackled, but the silence was deafening.

It was only about forty-five seconds, but seemed much longer before Rhonda finally broke the spell that was holding them.

"My fault. I'm sorry for pushing you, Beca." She looked directly at her friend as she continued, "I know if you have something you wish to share you will do it in your own time. I certainly don't want to jeopardize our friendship, so please forgive me."

Before Beca could answer, Jillian butted in, admitting she had also overstepped the boundaries and asked for forgiveness.

Normally Beca was compassionate, but they had made her uncomfortable. She wanted just a moment of revenge, so she did not answer immediately, letting the emotional guilt give discipline to her prying friends. Still staring into the fire, the scheme backfired on Beca, who was now feeling guilty for mistreating those who cared about her.

"I forgive you," she stated, relieving both Jillian and Rhonda that she had not only spoken but had forgiven them.

"All right," said Rhonda, getting up. "Now maybe we can get started cooking our evening meal. I've been looking forward to cooking those steaks and baked potatoes over the open fire."

Still staring into the fire, Beca made another comment simply saying, "There is another."

Jillian—slightly confused—asked, "Another what?"

This time Beca looked directly at Jillian and responded with a smirk on her face, "Another guy."

Jillian looked quickly at Rhonda, who seemed just as shocked as she felt. Neither one was sure how to respond, especially after what had just taken place. Rhonda sat back down, temporarily forgetting about the evening meal.

"Look," Beca began, "you need to cut me some slack here. I've had a couple of dates with Jason—the guy who totaled my car as I told you earlier today—and I've had a date with Peter—the guy I bought my new car from. But I assure you, it really is nothing, just a couple of harmless dates."

Rhonda looked directly into Beca's eyes, shaking her head. "You sly dog; you are holding out on us. I thought you showed some interest in that Peter guy. Do you really think we believe you went out with these guys just to be friends? Not for a second, and neither do you." She briefly stopped talking before asking, "Two at one time, Beca?

"All right," she responded, "I know I've held back on you guys, but I just didn't want anybody to be too hopeful. What if it doesn't work out? I'll have to explain, and the less people who know at this point, the better. So now I have told you as much as I'm going to, so please leave it at that."

Rhonda persisted with one more question, asking Beca if her parents knew.

She confessed she really hadn't told them much. "Enough of that," she blurted out, ending the topic. "Let's get that food cooking. I'm hungry."

The remainder of the evening flew by as they enjoyed food from the campfire. The crisp cool evening air was moving in with the setting sun. They let the fire die down and retired early, expecting to begin the morrow as soon as the sun allowed them to.

It was a brisk morning as the three emerged from the tent. Jillian was getting the fire started, with the remaining firewood Rhonda had collected the previous evening. Rhonda and Beca started preparing a pancake breakfast. "The fire feels so good," Jillian stated, standing close to its growing flame for warmth.

Beca told Rhonda that her idea for an early fall camping trip was inspired and looked like a success. She admitted, "I actually do enjoy being with my friends in the great outdoors, even with the cooler temperatures."

Rhonda suggested squeezing a short hike in after breakfast, emphasizing it was a good way to warm up, and they did have a few hours before they needed to head home. By late morning, with the hike complete, the three sat by the dying fire trying to hold onto a few more minutes of the weekend together. Regretfully, they finally packed up and headed back to Rhonda's house, where the other two had left their vehicles.

Driving to work Monday morning, Beca thought to herself, with the long holiday weekend last week and the campout this past weekend, hopefully things could get back to normal for a while. She was thinking about fall, with the changes coming, she congratulated herself for keeping up on the house since there were no major issues to deal with before winter.

She enjoyed summer, but her favorite season was fall with the crisp air and changing colors. She especially liked riding her bike in the fall season, she couldn't explain it but it gave her a sense of refreshment and freedom not felt during the other seasons.

Wednesday evening, after taking a short bike ride, Beca was relaxing with a bowl of popcorn when the phone rang. She realized as soon as she answered that it was Peter. He mentioned it had been a little while since their date. He then inquired how she was doing. She told him she was doing well and told him about spending Labor Day with her family and also about the past weekend of camping with her friends. Peter again informed her he had enjoyed the time they spent together a few weeks ago, cautiously asking if it was too soon for another evening together.

A TIME OF LEARNING

Beca could hear the anxiety in Peter's voice when asking her for another date. So she decided to put him at ease as soon as possible. Indicating her interest, she asked, "What did you have in mind?"

"Well," he said, "If you don't mind, I promised my daughter, Ruth, an afternoon trip to a cider mill sometime this fall and thought maybe you could come along with us. It would be a half hour ride to get there. They have horse-drawn wagon rides and a few other fall activities to enjoy. We plan to stop at a kid-friendly restaurant on the way back." He waited momentarily for her response.

Beca knew this was really a test to find out who she was and what she liked to do.

"That does sound like an exciting change of pace, and I would like to meet your daughter," she said.

"All right," he replied. "They are just getting started for the year, so I called you rather early hoping we could make plans to go a week from Saturday. Say we pick you up at three in the afternoon?"

Beca thought quickly, trying to remember if there were any conflicts before responding with a cheerful, "That works. I'll figure on it."

Not prolonging the conversation, Peter abruptly replied, "Good! I will see you then." He hung up.

There was still one fall project Beca needed to take care of that actually gave her enjoyment during the winter months. She had a fireplace in her home and liked to use it occasionally on those cold winter evenings, so she needed to get her annual supply of firewood. She always took the easy way and bought it already cut, split, and delivered. Searching the paper for wood, she found a nice mix of cherry and oak for a reasonable price. She called and placed her order to be delivered on Saturday.

Thursday evening Beca gave her friend Lisa a call and set a coffee date with her for Saturday evening, telling her she felt it was time to have a good girl talk. Saturday morning she woke at her usual time, looked at her clock and rolled back over trying to get a little more sleep in on her day off. She dozed for a while but the wind was buffeting the house, bringing a storm in, so she finally got up. She told Missy it would be nice if the weather cooperated with the weekends.

She remembered the firewood delivery was coming today, sometime late morning, to be unloaded and stacked by hand, regardless of the weather. She got herself a bowl of cold cereal and sat down in the living room and turned on the television thinking, *What a rotten day. I just don't seem to have much energy, so maybe I'll just do nothing today.*

Beca woke up as Missy jumped on her lap. Startled by the intrusion on her sleep, she wondered what time it was and how long she had been asleep. It was mid morning already, and she had not even gotten dressed yet. She knew the firewood delivery could be there at any time, so she hurriedly dressed into some grubby clothes. Looking outside, she was happy to see the rain had already passed, but it had left everything quite wet.

Missy kept following Beca through the house until it finally dawned on her that she had forgotten to feed her last night. Maybe that's why she woke her up in the first place. "I'm sorry, Missy," she said while giving an extra portion to make amends.

Just a few minutes later there was a knock on the door; the firewood had arrived. She immediately went outside to help unload the cargo.

After the delivery guy left, Beca headed straight for the shower. She not only had sweat from the workout but also was chilled to the bone at the same time, and a warm shower was very inviting.

The shower felt so good she didn't want to get out, she was glad the outing with Peter was next week. The only plans she had for today was meeting Lisa later that evening. After the shower she curled up in her favorite chair in the living room with a book and said out loud, "I really could use that fire now."

The coffee shop was inviting, after the dreary day. Beca entered to find Lisa already there sitting in a booth. As she approached the booth Lisa said, "I already placed my order, so you might want to place yours before sitting down."

After ordering a large caramel latte, Beca sat down in the booth and let out a big sigh. Lisa was a good listener, maybe that's why she felt comfortable talking to her. Lisa remarked after hearing the big sigh from her friend, "So, I'm guessing you either had a hard day or are you just feeling blah with the gloomy weather."

She replied, "It's just been one of those days, I guess nothing really. I just can't seem to get on top of it. Maybe my hot latte will help."

"Well, you got me here now," Lisa stated, letting Beca know she was all ears. Then boldly asked, "So what's happening in your life that we need to discuss?"

The coffees arrived, giving Beca a reprieve. They thanked the deliverer and each took a sip of their hot beverage.

"Well," she began, "I don't really have anything concrete to tell you or ask your opinion on. I've had a date with Peter, one guy, and a few with Jason, the other guy. I've been careful to space them out and I don't believe I have made any slip-ups. I guess I just needed someone to confide in, someone I can talk freely with instead of keeping it bottled up. I know my good friend Lisa is just that someone."

Lisa smiled at the compliment and simply said, "Thanks."

After each had again sampled her latte, Lisa asked, "What are you looking for? Be blunt with me, a husband? Some guy friends? A change of pace in life?"

Then she held her tongue waiting for her friend to digest the questions that she had boldly asked.

"What happened to listening?" Beca inquired of Lisa, before she admitted to asking herself those same questions. "Well, I always wanted to marry and have a family of my own," she confessed. "You and I both know we get set in our ways, and I've learned to be happy alone. I've got my house, a job I enjoy, friends, family, and even my hobby of riding bike, which I find quite fulfilling and can do that alone too."

Lisa scolded Beca, "I know I'm supposed to be the listener here, but as a friend, I'm going to say it straight out. You are not that old yet. You're an attractive woman, and you've got energy with enthusiasm for life. I believe the only reason you don't have more men banging on your door is because you're hiding. I'll leave it at that."

Beca blinked rapidly a few times pondering what Lisa had just said so bluntly.

Lisa couldn't leave it at that, so she added, "I care about you as my friend, I want the very best for you, and I don't believe for a minute that you have given up on the family idea."

Neither spoke immediately; they continued drinking their coffees, each deep in her thoughts. Beca broke the silence by sighing then said, "Lisa, you are right. I guess maybe I lost some hope as time passed. You know I'm not a quitter, and we should all continue having dreams regardless of our age. Thanks for being a friend who listens and encourages, but I gotta tell ya, I was starting to get upset with your bold remarks."

With a broad smile, Lisa replied, "It was a risk I was willing to take."

They both laughed as they slowly finished their coffees. A few minutes later, they headed for the door to go their separate ways.

The ride home gave Beca time to mull over the remarks Lisa had made. It was not exactly the evening of talking she had envisioned, but in a sense it was. She knew Lisa had seen through her and was right in her assumptions, now she needed to convince herself. She spoke out loud as if someone else were telling her the issue. *Beca, you do know what you want—you have always wanted it. You're just scared of letting someone in. It is better to have loved and lost than to never have loved at all. Now be big enough to admit it, then you go for it, girl.* The personal reprimand seemed to be effective, or maybe it was the caffeine from the coffee. It didn't matter, now she was totally convinced the future was hers for the taking.

As Beca placed her head on the pillow that night she reviewed how her day had played out, it had started slowly and rough, maybe even slightly confusing. But it had changed to a positive attitude with clear direction. She smiled as she happily dozed off expecting happy dreams.

Sunday afternoon Beca retrieved a message left by Jason while she was in church that morning. He confessed that maybe the kiss he had surprised her with at the end of their date was premature in their relationship. He confessed feeling he may have offended her and now wanted to apologize. Then added, "I'll give you whatever space you need. Please call me when you're ready."

Yes, the kiss was a surprise, she thought, but it had not bothered her. She erased the message, deciding not to call just yet.

The beginning of the week brought a few warm days—almost an Indian summer, but the weather report showed much cooler by Friday. *Good*, she thought in anticipation, *it will make for a better time at the cider mill with Peter and his daughter, Ruth, on Saturday.*

It wasn't until she was leaving work on Friday that Beca remembered she had not called Jason back concerning his plea of forgiveness. She had not purposefully waited, but maybe she subconsciously did, hoping to slow Jason down, giving Peter a chance. Shortly after arriving home, Beca called Jason to set things right. He answered after the third ring with apprehension in his voice. She tried to smooth things over with the "I've been so busy lately" phrase, Jason was only too happy to accept it. She cut Jason off before he could ask anything, quickly telling him she had another busy weekend coming up, then suggested he call next week before saying a hasty "good-bye."

Saturday Beca woke in anticipation of the outing with Peter. She wondered what his daughter was like and how it all was going to work out today. She knew she needed to keep herself busy all day or the waiting would drive her insane. The cooler temperatures had already moved in, the thermometer read only fifty degrees, at eight in the morning. *It might warm up some*, she thought. But right now it was just too chilly for yard work, so she spent the first couple of hours cleaning inside the house.

By late morning Beca was trying to decide how to keep herself busy for the next few hours. She did need to get a few groceries and thought maybe she should stop by her parents' house for a short visit. She called her mother to let her know she would be dropping by then made herself presentable to go out in public before leaving the house.

Stopping at her parents' home first, Beca allotted herself a certain amount of time to be there. She did need the groceries, and she still wanted time to get ready for the outing before Peter showed up this afternoon. As she entered the house her mother commented she had timed it just right because lunch was ready. She then asked Beca if she wanted coffee to drink with the meal. Beca looked sheepish as she confessed she had actually forgotten about lunch but admitted she was getting hungry, especially after working hard cleaning the house all morning.

Her father joined the two ladies as they all sat down for lunch. He offered a word of thanks for the food and the many blessings the family enjoyed each day. Elaine got up from the table to retrieve the coffee pot from the kitchen counter; placing it on the table, she looked at her husband and commented, "Yes, honey, it's a fresh pot."

Beca smiled, knowing how her father relished fresh coffee; he didn't like it even an hour old.

During the noon meal, they talked about current events and activities in each of the family members' lives. Beca mentioned how busy life seemed lately, prompting Elaine to ask her daughter what was keeping her so busy. She responded, "You know, vacations, yard work, holidays, the camping trip with Rhonda and Jillian, and getting ready for the upcoming winter months."

With just the three of them sitting there, Beca's father listened carefully to his daughter. As she spoke he processed what was being said, and he remembered the Labor Day family gathering. She had mentioned spending time with a friend, but clammed up quickly when Jake had questioned who it was. His wife had also indicated to him she felt Beca was hiding something lately but she didn't know what.

With a break in the conversation, Josh put down his coffee, cleared his throat, and looked directly at his daughter. He asked bluntly, "Beca, is there a guy in your life you've been keeping from us?"

Her face felt warm. She had not expected such a direct question, especially from her father. She stuttered as she began, "I...I...ah. Well, maybe there is someone, but it really is nothing at this point. I really don't want to discuss it." She grabbed her sandwich and proceeded to take a huge bite, indicating she had no intention of saying anything else. She glanced over at her mother who had a faint smile on her face.

Beca helped her mother clean up after the lunch then left sooner than she had initially intended. Not really looking for anything, she wandered through a few stores at the mini mall next to the grocery store, just trying to waste the extra time she now felt she had. Arriving home with almost an hour before Peter was to pick her up, Beca brought the groceries in and put them away before heading to the shower.

How do I dress for an outdoor adventure? she asked herself. *I need to be practical, but at the same time I have to look good.* She chose a flannel shirt and a newer pair of blue jeans, thinking practical overrules looks when outside in the cooler fall temperatures. *Besides, I'll be wearing a jacket. I certainly don't like being cold.*

Beca heard a racket out in her yard and asked out loud in a voice of desperation, "Now what?"

It was almost time for Peter to show up, and she didn't have time to deal with anything else right now. Looking out the window to find the cause of the racket, she was surprised to see it was Peter, who had pulled into her drive. She went out to meet him, bewildered by the startling situation.

As he was getting out of his car he noticed her immediately. She had exited the house and, with a look of dismay written all over her face, approached him. Peter spoke first, sheepishly explaining, "My car seems to have lost its muffler. It came off a few miles back, and I didn't want to worry you by being late." Then he added, "I hope this isn't an indication of how our time together will be today."

Beca—over the initial shock—shivered, realizing she had run out of the house without her jacket. She quickly said, "It's cold out here. Get Ruth out of the car and come inside so we can figure out what to do." Then she turned and went back into the house where it was warm.

Now she was glad that she had cleaned her house that morning, this was an unexpected development. She opened the door for Ruth as she approached the house with her father right behind her. Upon entering, Ruth looked up at Beca and said, "Thank you," instantly melting Beca's heart. Peter apologized by saying, "I knew the muffler was getting bad, just not that bad. Now I've ruined the day for you, and I can only imagine the impression I've made."

"The day is not ruined," she assured Peter. "I have a very nice car we can take this afternoon if you're all right with that. Maybe we can drop your car off at the muffler shop and get it fixed while we are gone."

Peter looked at Beca with new respect, making a mental note of her practicality and calmness in a sticky situation. He replied, "That is a great idea...if we can find a place open on Saturday afternoon."

She quickly retrieved a phone book and handed it to Peter, saying, "Maybe we can change your luck."

He gladly accepted the challenge and proceeded to look for a repair shop in the phone book as she handed him the phone to make a few calls.

Peter found a shop a couple of miles out of their way, but they were open until five and said they could still get it done today. He looked at Beca before leaving the house and commented, "I know this is awkward, and I appreciate your willingness. This is really embarrassing for me, but can I ask a favor?"

She was intrigued and replied, "Sure."

He asked if Ruth could ride with her to the repair shop while he drove the noise-mobile alone. It brought a smile to Beca's face as she replied, "I'd be honored."

He proceeded to transfer the car seat into her car and strapped Ruth into it.

It was only about six or seven miles to the repair shop, but in that short time Beca learned Ruth was not shy and liked to talk. Ruth was curious, asking her everything from where they were going and why she was riding with her to "Did you know my mommy?" Beca was ready for Peter to join by the time they arrived at the muffler repair shop, although she did enjoy answering the little girl's many questions.

Getting into her car, Peter again thanked her, saying, "I owe you big for helping me today."

She did not reply to his comment but inquired when the car would be done and if he could drive it home tonight. He replied, "They were very helpful by giving me an upfront cost, which I already paid. When it is finished they will put the receipt inside with the key on the tire, so we should be all set."

He then gave directions to Beca for the cider mill as he timidly admitted that this was not the picture he had in mind of their time together today. She confessed she too had expected something different but added, "It will all work out." Looking over at Peter, she asked, "Did you know Ruth is talkative and full of questions?"

"Yes, I know," he replied in a matter of fact way. "She likes to know what's going on and who everybody is." He turned to look back at Ruth who was oblivious to the adults talking; she was looking out the window and humming to herself.

En route to the cider mill, Peter told Beca he was impressed with the nice house she had. Complimenting that it seemed to have just the right amount of landscaping to give it character. She was flattered he had noticed it at all with the distracting activities of the day, so she questioned him, "Do you get into landscaping?"

He replied with an enthusiastic "I do. I love the smells and the joy a beautiful yard brings. It's always a real mood lifter, and I guess you could say it's sort of a hobby of mine to putter in the yard."

The half hour drive went quickly as they talked comfortably together. Finding a parking place at the mill was a challenge not only because it was busy, but also the only spots left were in the mud. Beca stopped in the main drive and instructed Peter to get out with Ruth so she could go park in the mud. "No use all of us getting muddy feet," she stated.

He agreed, suggesting he park the car while she stayed with Ruth.

"No time for that," she said. "I'm holding up traffic."

So Peter got out and took Ruth out of the back seat of the Nissan, before Beca went to park.

It was light jacket weather as the three took a horse-drawn wagon ride through the orchard. Ruth was fascinated by the horses and couldn't care less about the scenery her father was pointing out. Beca was slightly envious of Ruth as Peter held his daughter close, giving her all the attention during the ride, but she was also impressed with the relationship he had with her.

She thought he was a good father. She also noticed how much little Ruth adored her father.

After the ride, they went inside to see how the apple cider was made. It interested the adults more than it did Ruth, who kept asking if they could go for another horsy ride. Peter stooped down by his daughter and held her by the shoulders, getting her attention, he gently said, "Remember what Daddy talked to you about before we left home? How we are spending time with Beca today, and we need to do things she likes too?"

"Okay, Daddy," Ruth replied. "But can we go on another horsy ride before we go?"

Beca, hearing the dialogue, turned her head so Ruth could not see her smile because of her persistence.

Peter answered his daughter as he stood up simply saying, "We will see."

They spent an hour looking around, especially at the small animal farm they had there for kids to enjoy. Ruth reminded her father that she still wanted another horsy ride, to which he conceded. Before leaving, they went into the mill store for a look around. Peter decided to buy a gallon of cider while Beca picked out a couple of knick-knacks for her house.

Beca drove the car out of the mud hole where she had parked, allowing Peter and Ruth to get in on dry ground. They had not even gotten to the road before Ruth, whining slightly, asked, "Are we going to eat now? I'm hungry."

Peter, glancing at his watch, said in a surprised manner, "It's almost six o'clock, no wonder Ruth is hungry. If it's all right with you, Beca, maybe we can find a fast food restaurant nearby and stop for dinner."

Keeping her eyes on her driving, she responded, "Ruth isn't the only one hungry."

The cool weather and being out in it created good appetites. Peter ordered a kid's meal for Ruth, but during the meal she kept asking for some of his to supplement it. Beca noticed Peter had ordered two sandwiches for himself, so she did the same, almost feeling guilty, but hunger had won out over guilt.

On the ride home, Ruth fell asleep, and Beca commented how full of life she had been all day. She was glad they had taken Ruth along. Getting to know her was fun and very interesting.

Peter reminded Beca they needed to go to the muffler shop to retrieve his car. He told her he hated to end their time together but that he should head home directly from the repair shop. Ruth needed a bath tonight so she was ready for church tomorrow. He asked Beca if she attended church, and if she did, where?

She replied, "I go almost every week to the Bible church I was raised in."

At the repair shop, the car was done with the keys on the tire and receipt inside as expected. Peter transferred Ruth into his car while she was slowly waking from her groggy state of sleep. With Ruth in the car, Peter turned his attention to Beca, who was standing beside the car admiring Ruth. He asked her if he could give her a hug. She did not answer but held her arms out in response; they briefly hugged. Taking a step back after the hug, Peter took a deep breath and said, "I really like you and desire to continue this relationship, I know we have only dated a couple of times but I feel a connection with you. Today with the difficulties we had, I saw who you are and feel comfortable with you, especially when I watched you with Ruth." Then he finished by saying, "Thank you for today. Hopefully we can spend more time together in the future."

Beca got in her car while Peter waited for her to leave before he did.

Sunday morning, Beca woke with a pounding headache, getting up only long enough to take four aspirin before crawling back into bed. Finally emerging a few hours later, she made a cup of coffee and got a bowl of cold cereal to satisfy the hunger pains. The headache was now just a bearable dull pain as Beca sat down in her living room, still in her pajamas. As soon as she sat down, Missy tried to jump up on her lap, but she was not in the mood and quickly pushed her away so she could eat her late breakfast.

The television was on, but Beca was in a zombie state—not really paying attention to it, only wishing the headache would just go away. She wondered if she was paying a price for allowing herself a good time yesterday. She could hear the wind blowing outside, so she flipped the television on to the weather channel to see what they guessed might happen today. It appeared another cold front was coming in with maybe even a few showers, making her feel under the weather even more, so she pulled a blanket over her legs for warmth.

The phone rang and Beca struggled to get to it in time from her comfortable position. It was her mother checking up because she had not seen her in church. She informed her mom of her condition, before assuring her she would be better by tomorrow.

Monday she felt much better and arrived at work as usual. It didn't take long before one of her coworkers asked, "So Beca, you had a good weekend, uh?"

"What?" she inquired. "Why do you say that?"

Well, he replied, "Someone seems in a pretty good mood for a Monday."

She explained about being under the weather yesterday and now she was just making up for it.

He responded with, "Yeah, whatever," and walked away.

SEASONS OF LIFE

Almost a full week went by, and Jason had not called. In one way it gave Beca some breathing room, but she wondered if she had offended him when she informed him a week ago how busy she was.

She called Lisa Thursday evening to bounce the thoughts of anxiety off her friend. Lisa listened as she shared how she was short with Jason then blurted out, "Now either he's given up, or he's playing a game with me."

"Beca, Beca, Beca," Lisa said sharply, "just chill. You are so paranoid. Give it time; don't make assumptions. It will all play out. Remember how you went on vacation without keeping someone informed?"

"Yes," Beca replied. "I guess I did do that, and now you have reminded me of another reason to believe Jason is gun shy." She sighed in desperation.

"No, no, no," Lisa shot back. "He does understand; that's what I'm trying to tell you. He's giving you the room you need right now, so give him a chance."

"Thanks for the reality check, she humbly replied. I know I can count on you as a friend who always gives it to me straight; you know that's why I call you."

It was the first weekend in October, the first one in some time that Beca had no plans. After sleeping in late on Saturday she finally decided she had better do something productive, so she forced herself to emerge from the bedroom. After the usual house chores, she went outside to a partly cloudy day and spent the rest of the morning doing yard work. She knew it was time to start winterizing the yard, so she mowed the lawn before trimming down the flowerbeds, then she stored the water hoses in the garage.

Beca had lived in Michigan long enough to know when the cold decided to come, it usually came quickly. So when the opportunity was there to prepare, you had better take it. Happy to have completed the yard preparation for the coming winter, she went inside to get lunch. As she ate in solitude she wondered what she could fill the rest of the day with. After thinking of a few possibilities, she decided to go biking while the weather was still somewhat warm. Loading her bike onto the car rack, Beca thought she would go back to the trail she had sprained her wrist on. The rain that day had kept her from exploring much.

The trail was almost abandoned compared to the last time she had been there. During the first mile on the trail, she saw a couple of walkers and a father biking with his two young sons that needed plenty of room. The air was cool, but Beca had prepared for it with her jeans, T-shirt, another shirt, and a jacket. She was comfortable, even with the trees along the path blocking whatever sunlight there was that day. It brought a smile to her face when she noticed the leaves had already changed color, making the ride enjoyable as the continually changing colorful scenery passed by.

Careful to watch the trail as well as looking around at the scenery, she dodged a couple of potholes—not wanting a repeat of the incident with the previous ride on this trail. Sometimes it was difficult to see the trail because the trees were beginning to drop a few leaves, covering some of the pavement. *Thankfully it's not raining or wet this time,* she told herself. If it were, the leaves might be slippery, creating another hazard. After biking for a couple of hours, the trail she was following came to a small town with a few shops that enticed her, so she convinced herself—without too much trouble—she needed a break. She stopped and padlocked her bike to a pole, before setting off on foot to explore the nearby shops.

The break lasted longer than Beca had anticipated. After checking out the small town shops, she grabbed a bite to eat. Looking at her watch, she knew it was time to head back, but she made a mental note to continue exploring the trail from this point some other time. The temperatures started dropping as she headed back to her car, two hours away. When she finally arrived at the original point of the day's adventure, it was already starting to get dark. Beca was cold, despite the warm clothing and energy exerted during the ride. She loaded the bike quickly as a breeze was starting to come up with the setting of the sun. Once loaded, she headed home, looking forward to a hot shower.

Following the soothing warm shower, Beca started her first fire since last winter in the fireplace. The recently purchased cherry and oak wood filled the house with its natural aroma while giving extra warmth to the living room. She made herself a bowl of popcorn and curled up in her favorite chair, placing a book on the table next to her. Before reading, she watched the flames dancing upward, eagerly absorbing the heat while indulging in the popcorn.

Losing herself in thought for a few minutes, Beca reflected on all the good that had happened in her life over the past few months. She thought about Thanksgiving being just around the corner but knew she need not wait for the holiday; she was thankful for the way things had been. Now things were happening in her life that were not only exciting but also could bring positive changes if she desired. "That's right, if I desire," she said out loud. And for a brief moment, she felt in control before again talking out loud asking herself, "What do you really want, Beca? What do you really want?" Her eyes were glazed over as she stared into the flames of the fire while she continued eating the popcorn.

The fire was slowly dying down, so she got up and added more wood to it. She wanted to enjoy the smells, sounds, and warmth of it for a while longer, maybe in a few minutes getting lost in the world of reading. After that she would hit the sack.

She had friends and family that cared for her. Beca liked her job, home, and church, these were all comfortable and satisfying, she thought as she continued to reflect on her existing life. She asked herself once again out loud, "What do you really want?" Finally she picked her book up to read for the remainder of her Saturday evening.

Sunday. Monday. Tuesday. Still no call from Jason. The silence provoked Beca into wondering if he really was offended by some of her actions, even if he didn't admit it. She remembered the advice from Lisa to give it time, *but time,* she reasoned, *can drive people apart as well. Whoever said time makes the heart fonder? Does that include uncertainty?* She thought about calling Jason just to find out where he stood on the issue, but her common sense told her not to make any moves out of irrational thinking. So she did nothing beyond driving herself crazy with mind games by creating possible scenarios.

The clouds had turned a deep blue, and the winds were bringing the first blast of cold winter air in on Friday. Her coworkers had been talking about how it looked like an early winter this year. Beca thought it was normal, and they were just voicing their opinion in hopes of holding onto the warmer season a little longer.

At home Missy welcomed her like a long lost friend, making her believe the cat knew winter was coming. She told Missy not to worry because it was just the first wave of cold air, and they probably wouldn't see any snow for at least another month or two. Missy seemed to understand and went off to find a cozy place for a catnap.

Just after getting a pan out to make a spaghetti dinner, the phone rang. "Finally," she said so loudly she surprised herself. She made her way to the phone, thinking Jason had finally come to his senses. Picking up the phone, with the spaghetti pan still in her hand, Beca answered with a soft almost sweet, "Hello." The voice on the other end quickly replied in a brash manner. "Well, I guess you were expecting some other call because you have never talked to me that way before."

Realizing what she had done and to whom she had done it to, Beca boldly stated, "I got ya, Rhonda!"

Rhonda laughed at her and replied, "Oh, no you didn't. I know you better than that. So which guy was it you were expecting a call from? Come clean now, you've already been caught."

She knew she could not convince Rhonda otherwise, so she admitted maybe she was expecting a call from someone else, quickly trying to change the topic of discussion by asking, "So if I am expecting a call, don't you think we better leave this line available?"

"All right," Rhonda conceded, giving in. "I just called to see if you had some time available tomorrow. I thought we should spend some time together, maybe hit a few antique shops followed by some over priced café for a light lunch and lattes, just the two of us."

Beca wondered if Rhonda was curious whether anything had happened with her relationships and was going to use the outing to pry for an update. She really wasn't too concerned because she felt she had enough self-control to give only the information she desired to. Besides, she reasoned, it looked like a boring weekend, so antiquing and a café with lattes sounded like a nice change of pace. She agreed to pick Rhonda up at ten thirty the next morning.

Beca had taken no more than three steps from the phone when she was summoned back to it. Not wanting to make the same mistake answering it like she had done with Rhonda, she spoke a hello with no particular emotion connected to it. This time it was Jason. As soon as she recognized his voice, she softened hers to put him at ease, stating, "I was just thinking about you."

Jason, still apprehensive from the previous weeks of sporadic conversations, was taken back momentarily by her remark. Gaining back his composure, he asked if everything was going well for her lately, and if she might possibly be available to spend an evening with him in the near future. She replied "That is a good possibility. What did you have in mind?"

Jason hesitated before he said, "I really was not sure if you were interested in me. I kinda felt like I was getting the cold shoulder, so I must admit I didn't have anything preplanned, I was just hoping you'd say yes."

Suddenly she was speechless and even felt slightly sick. She had not intentionally given that impression and yet unintentionally maybe she did. Her mind and mouth were not connecting, and she perceived the deafening silence was sending a message.

You must answer soon, she told herself. *He is waiting for something, anything.*

Jason spoke before she put her thoughts into words by asking, "Beca, just be honest with me right up front. Is there anything between us? Do we have something here or not? Look," he continued, "I'm in, and I need to know if you are, or if I'm just chasing my tail." Then he again waited for her to tell him what the next step was going to be.

Beca tried choosing her words carefully as she replied to his inquiries. "Jason," she began in a submissive tone to ease the tension, "I do want to spend more time with you. I really have been busy over the past month, and as I told you previously, I do want to take things slow. I don't know if anything will work between us, but we can never find out if we don't try. I still want to try."

Then she suggested they have another dinner at The Barn together, mentioning she had enjoyed the place and the company she was with. "Maybe," she added, "we can catch a movie afterward, just like last time." She concluded by suggesting, "I have both Friday and Saturday open next week, if that works for you?"

Jason, now relaxed slightly, was satisfied with the suggestion and possible continuation of the relationship replied, "Next Friday. I'll pick you up at six."

She agreed, but before Jason let her hang up, he said that maybe he had jumped to conclusions and apologized for his attitude.

Beca slowly hung the phone up. Her head was still spinning from the idea she gave Jason reason to question their relationship. Looking down, she noticed that she was still hanging onto the spaghetti pan, reminding her of what she had intended to do before the phone sidetracked her.

The next morning she was driving toward Rhonda's house for the anticipated antiquing together. Singing with the CD player, she was in a good mood and was enjoying the crisp morning air. As Rhonda was getting into the car she couldn't help but notice Beca's smile and cheery mood, so she asked, "Are you ready to shop?"

Beca was quick to respond with an upbeat response. "Oh yeah, I even brought money, so let's go. Get in girl," she demanded.

They both laughed as she backed her car out of the driveway and turned toward town.

The morning flew as the two friends chatted while browsing the stores that were filled with interesting items from days gone by. They laughed at some things, making comments like one person's junk is another's treasure, however they were awestruck or mystified by some of the other items they saw. Both ended up spending more than they had allotted themselves, finding treasures at prices too good to pass up, to decorate their homes with things they didn't need. Beca found a miniature wagon, a milk bottle, and a picture. Rhonda really liked a desk she found but concluded her husband might have an issue with the price if she bought it, especially if she told him he needed to go pick it up. So she settled for a Tiffany lamp that had caught her eye and a vase so large Beca told her she could grow a tree in it.

Entering a café for lunch, Rhonda mentioned it better be a light lunch for both of them after the mini-spending spree they had over the past couple of hours. The café was not busy because the friends had been so into antiquing, the normal lunch hour crowd had already left. Beca told Rhonda even if she spent more then she figured she might, there was no way she was going to forfeit the latte.

Sitting with lattes and sandwiches before them, Rhonda asked for the personal life update, just like Beca knew she would. Previously on the campout, she had held back some but now with new developments taking place, she felt some of the excitement needed to be shared with her close friend.

She gave her friend the highlights of her date with Peter, including how she ended up driving due to the muffler issue with Peter's car. She indicated she had enjoyed the day and told how his daughter, Ruth, was talkative but seemed to listen well to her father. Then she told about having another date with Jason, coming up next Friday with a meal and movie night.

Rhonda finished her sandwich, but Beca had hardly touched hers because she had been doing all the talking. She finally got back to her sandwich as Rhonda sipped the remainder of her latte; both sat silently for a full minute.

"Beca," Rhonda began, "thanks for sharing with me. I really do enjoy being part of your life. I will not give you advice unless you ask for it, but I got to tell you, girl"—she continued with a smirk on her face—"any girl would be envious of you right now, with two guys at the same time. You have got it going on!" Then she stopped short, checking her words before speaking again. "Be careful, men can be jealous, and if they find out about each other, you could lose both of them." Covering herself she added, "That's not advice just an observation."

Beca nodded her head in understanding but made no further comment.

Arriving home Beca unloaded her treasures. She placed the miniature wagon in the corner of the living room, next to the fireplace, removing the plastic planter that had been sitting there. She also placed the milk bottle on the mantel. Standing back, she observed the décor change and congratulated herself for making it look homey.

She took another look at the picture she had purchased, it was a hand painted scene of a farm with wild flowers in the surrounding green pastures. Not sure why she bought it, Beca concluded it didn't fit anywhere, at least not right now, so she slipped it into a closet to be reviewed at a later time.

Walking to her car after work Friday evening, Beca observed how good the warm sunshine felt. The week had gone by without incident, and tonight Jason was taking her to The Barn restaurant again, just like she had suggested the last time they talked. She had an hour between work and Jason picking her up, giving her plenty of time to get ready for the evening.

The drive home took twenty minutes including the stop for fuel on the way. Exiting the bathroom, after a longer than usual shower, she heard the phone ring, so she made a mad dash to catch the caller before they had a chance to hang up.

It was an unexpected call from Peter who asked if it was too late to ask her out for dinner that evening, also telling her she had been on his mind all day. She surprised herself by calmly replying, "I'm sorry Peter, but I already have plans for this evening." Glancing at the clock she saw she had less than five minutes before Jason was picking her up, and she still needed to finish getting ready.

Peter was not satisfied to leave the call with the answer he received, so he inquired about tomorrow evening. Beca wasn't sure she was ready for back-to-back dates with two different men, so she lied—telling him her weekend was already booked. Then she boldly asked if they could plan ahead to next weekend, giving him hope; and her, space. He asked if she minded having Ruth come along with them.

She bluntly told him that as much as she had enjoyed Ruth along last time, she felt the relationship required time alone, time to talk on a more personal level.

The doorbell rang, and Beca jumped, she had not heard Jason pull into her drive. Peter voiced that he had heard the doorbell, indicating he had better let her go and hung up in her ear before she could object. She was upset the conversation had not ended properly. Now Peter and next weekend were in limbo, however, she did not have time right now to deal with it. Jason rang the doorbell a second time. She went to the door, asking him to step in for a moment while she finished getting ready.

Missy came to greet Jason by rubbing against his legs while he was standing in the kitchen observing Beca's home. When she emerged a few minutes later, Jason commented, "I didn't know you had a cat. I'm allergic to them."

She did not respond to the remark but calmly said, "I'm all set, so let's go check out The Barn again. I'm so hungry I'm willing to eat in one."

Jason laughed briefly as he told her she had an interesting sense of humor.

On the way to the restaurant, Beca was absorbed in her thoughts pertaining to the abrupt ending to the phone call with Peter. Jason, sensing the quietness, looked over at her and asked, "Is something wrong?"

She was quickly brought back to the present by his question and answered with a lie, "No, I just had a hard day at work today."

He smiled at her, replying, "You did seemed rushed when I picked you up tonight." Then he instructed her to take a deep breath and relax the rest of the evening.

She replied, "You are so right. It is the weekend, and it's time to unwind and relax."

When he glanced over at her, she gave him a smile to complete the mood and confirm her words. She began to wonder when she had resorted to lying; now she had misled both Peter and Jason to cover up the dangerous but exciting game she found herself playing.

They were seated just a couple tables over from the last time they visited The Barn. They first placed drink orders of milk, just like before, but opted to order in a few minutes. Looking over the menu closer this time, both were impressed with the large selection. Beca told Jason it was easier to order when they were in a hurry, now they had too much time to change their minds. When the drinks arrived they were ready and placed their orders before starting any in-depth conversations.

Jason was going to take the bull by the horns to find out whom this lady really was; somehow he felt she was using him but hid any indication of his thoughts from her. He thought she was keeping him at a distance by holding back, if the relationship was going to grow he felt they needed to be open to each other. Now he needed to convince her of it without being overbearing or aggressive, possibly pushing her in the opposite direction.

Searching her eyes as she placed a straw into her chocolate milk, Jason prodded himself with thoughts of, *it's now or never; it's just me and her for the next hour*.

She looked up to see Jason staring at her and questioned him with one word, "What?"

Jason knew it was his move and decided to ease into it but be bold enough to lay it on the line. *After all*, he reasoned, *this may be the last opportunity*.

"Beca," he started, "last time we sat here, I told you who I was. When you spoke of who you were, I only found out what you did and even questioned you for more of who you are, but you stopped short of revealing any real details concerning your true personality. If this relationship is going to grow, we both need to be open and learn to trust, so I'm asking right here, right now, tell me who you are—the real you. I want to know your likes, dislikes, frustrations, joys, dreams, and what makes you tick."

The food arrived, saving her from giving an immediate answer, but at the same time, it distracted her thoughts as she thanked the waitress and asked for another chocolate milk. After the waitress left, Beca pushed her luck as she tried to blow off Jason by replying, "There is plenty of time for those discussions later. Let's enjoy a few minutes eating while the food is still hot." She proceeded to cut her steak, hoping the situation would self-dissolve.

Jason was not amused by her candor but followed suit and began eating. He did not want to seem overbearing, but he was beginning to believe Beca was single for a reason. The reasons he surmised were honesty, commitment, and maybe even selfishness. They ate in silence, and Jason was now waiting patiently to see what Beca's response might be. She had no doubt that Jason wanted this relationship to move to the next level and soon.

The tension was building on both sides of the table as each had their agenda of expectations. Beca understood she needed and even desired more time to learn who Jason was. He wanted to know he wasn't pursuing a dead end. Beca finally put down her fork and as she looked directly at Jason blurted out, "I'm sorry Jason. I can't enjoy this meal until we talk this out."

He didn't even flinch at her abruptness but continued to eat looking at her in that, "well go ahead and talk" face. So she continued, "I'm sorry for snapping at you, Jason. We did go out to get to know each other, and I guess I have held back some, but I just don't want to rush into anything. She sat back in her seat and asked, "What are you looking for?"

Jason slowly wiped his mouth before talking. "Hopefully a wife, one who is honest, confident, caring, understanding, and good looking is high on the list too, but you have already passed that test with flying colors."

The tension eased as they began to talk and understand the other's personalities and motives in life. They were completely at ease and even smiling by the time the meal was complete. Beca had revealed more of who she was by telling Jason about her family, their love for each other, and the competitions they enjoyed together. She told him how in control and free she felt when riding her bike. He now felt a huge hurdle had been cleared and felt closer to her because of it.

En route to the movie, Beca suggested a comedy may be the best choice, referencing the fact they needed to laugh together after the bumpy start to the evening. Jason readily agreed.

Later at the movie he held his hand out to her, indicating he wished to hold hers. She smiled as she slipped her hand into his, he gave a slight squeeze as he whispered "thank you."

Heading back to her home after the movie, Beca wondered how awkward the good-bye at the door might be, remembering the last departure. Jason must also have been thinking about it because he asked if a good night kiss was permissible at the door this evening. Thankful he had been kind enough to ask instead of unexpectedly surprising her like last time she answered, "Because you asked so nicely, I will permit it." At that instant she thought she felt the car speed up slightly.

Once at the house, Jason almost tripped running around the car to open Beca's door. He was trying to be a gentleman, before walking her the short distance to her door. She unlocked the house before turning back toward Jason; they slowly embraced in their first real kiss. Neither spoke immediately afterward; holding the moment they just looked into each others eyes. Finally Jason took a step backward and whispered a faint "good-bye" before returning to his car.

CONFESSIONS

Saturday morning, while slurping down a bowl of cold cereal, Beca remembered the abrupt ending to the phone call with Peter from the night before, when Jason was picking her up for their date. She had totally set any thoughts of Peter aside since the call until now, probably because Jason had been the one to dominate her attention and thoughts. Now she wondered if he expected her to call back to complete the discussion. She remembered Lisa's advice of giving it time because it would all work out, so she made the choice to let it be, at least for a few days.

It was already mid morning before Beca had finished with a few chores around the house. It was one of the nicest days she had seen for a while, with the temperature predicted to hit sixty degrees and very little breeze. She thought this might be her last chance to do some biking before winter prevented it. Beca also reminded herself she had not visited her parents in a couple of weeks. She called her mom to ensure they were home, thinking she would kill two birds with one stone and ride her bike to her parents' house.

Beca had only ridden her bike to her parents' house once before, she didn't relish the idea of taking the busy roads or the steep grades the route subjected her to. When talking to her mom, she told her she should be there in time for lunch, calculating the ride to be about an hour. The late October ride still held color in the trees as she paced herself in the fall air. She was relieved to see traffic minimal, making the ride more enjoyable.

"Is lunch ready?" Beca called out as she entered her parents' house. Seeing her father first, she asked, "Where is mom?"

Josh Stone stopped walking, turned toward his daughter and commented, "It's really nice to see you too, Beca."

Sheepishly she said, "Hi, Dad. It's nice to see you." Then she buttered him up by saying in a submissive tone, "I love you, Dad. Josh, still looking at his daughter, spoke sarcastically, "Nice try, Beca." Then walked away while saying, "Your mother just went downstairs."

As the three sat by the dinner table, Beca decided maybe it was time for her parents to know about some of the developments in her personal life. "Mom, Dad," she began, "I've got something to tell you."

Elaine Stone butted in brashly, "It's about time. We knew you were involved with someone, but isn't this a bit rushed?"

Beca sighed as she slowly shook her head before responding. "Okay, we need some rules here first. Don't jump to conclusions, Mom!"

Josh quickly jumped in trying to defuse the already emotional setting by saying, "We are all ears, honey. Tell us what's on your mind." He calmly continued making his sandwich waiting for her to begin again.

"I value your opinion and have respect for both of you," she continued, "but we really do need some rules here. I know how worried parents can be over their children, so I'm asking you to just listen. I just want to inform you, that's all. Remember I have it all under control. You have taught me how to stand on my own two feet, so let me. I just don't want you to blow this out of proportion." Beca held her tongue as she scanned the faces of her parents. She momentarily waited to see what reaction might come at this point in her speech. Her mother's face showed a bit of shock, but her father nodded in understanding, so Beca continued.

"I mentioned a few weeks ago that there was a guy in my life. Well, actually there are two guys I have been seeing for a few months now. One is named Jason. He's the guy who totaled out my Buick. The other guy is Peter, who I bought my Nissan from. I guess you could say my accident has brought interesting changes into my life. Right now I don't know if anything will become of either relationship, but I am dating them both."

Beca's father raised his eyebrows and stopped eating. He just stared at his daughter intently, letting the information sink in. Her mother sat expressionless but continued to eat, glancing occasionally at her husband.

"There," Beca stated boldly, "now it's out. I know I may have shocked you slightly, so that's why I had to preface the information with rules, but like I told you, I have it under control. I really can't comment any further or give details at this time. I hope you understand." She started eating the sandwich she had already made, but the tension made it feel like time stood still while waiting for a reaction. Josh cleared his throat indicating he had something to say.

"Two guys?" he questioned. After waiting a few seconds for affect, he continued. "Well, we did raise you to be independent. We know you have good judgment, so we want you to know," he hesitated before finishing his thought, "we will always be here for you and will respect your decisions. Thanks for sharing with us."

He looked over at his wife to confirm her alliance, but knew her well enough to see by her expression that she didn't feel the same way. However, she held her tongue out of respect for both her husband and daughter. Josh suggested they find a new subject and enjoy their time together.

After lunch Beca spent an hour with her father by working in the yard, she helped him trim trees as well as cover a few plants for the anticipated winter ahead. Later she poked her head inside, letting her mother know she would see her at church tomorrow, expressing a final good-bye before starting for home on her bike. At home she put the bike away in the garage, still hoping or holding onto the idea she might be able to ride a few more times before winter.

Beca was pleasantly surprised when Peter called Sunday evening. She didn't think—after the way their last conversation had ended—it would be so soon. The first thing Peter asked, and rightfully so, was if she had time to talk. She assured him she had the remainder of the evening unscheduled and apologized for the interruption they encountered Friday.

Picking up from Friday's phone conversation, Peter stated, "Beca, you told me the end of this week you had no plans, so I thought—as busy as you seem to be—I'd better call early. I will honor your request for just the two of us and find a sitter for Ruth. Oh, by the way," he continued, "you must have made an impression on Ruth, she keeps asking me about you and talks a lot about our trip to the cider mill. What works better: Friday or Saturday?"

"Saturdays give me the most time," she replied. "I don't feel rushed or tired from my day at work."

"All right," Peter butted in, hardly giving her time to complete the sentence. "Can I pick you up a little early, say five o'clock? I have a special place I want to take you, and it requires a little driving time, but that allows us the privacy required for any in-depth talking."

Beca was intrigued with Peter's implication of a special place. She asked what she should wear to this special place, while agreeing to the five o'clock time. Peter told her to wear something casual but nice and to be sure she had good walking shoes and a jacket.

They talked for another fifteen minutes about nothing in particular; they both enjoyed hearing the other's voice, and neither wanted to end the call. Beca finally used Missy as an excuse, claiming her cat was into something and needed immediate attention. Peter agreed to let her go as he reminded her of their five o'clock date on Saturday.

The plumbing supply store where Beca worked had a steady to heavy workload. She was grateful because it kept her from having time to think of anything else. It was five o'clock on Friday, with another week in the history books, when she left work. On the way home she cashed her paycheck, stopped at the grocery store, and had the oil changed in her car. She swung through the drive thru for a sub sandwich, telling herself it was a treat for working hard all week.

Groceries put away, sandwich devoured, and Missy taken care of, Beca prepared herself a soothing warm bubble bath. She chose a CD to have background music while soaking away the cares and stresses of life. Relaxing in the tub, she congratulated herself for putting Peter off until Saturday. She was happy to just take care of a few things on the way home, and have tonight to unwind with nothing demanding her time.

Peter was a few minutes early Saturday evening, but Beca was ready and anticipated an interesting evening with him, still wondering what he had planned. She asked him in a joking way if his car was going to fall apart, because he had indicated they needed to go some distance that evening.

Laughing lightly, he said, "You are not only beautiful but witty."

The comment made her spirits soar as he held the car door for her to get in.

Peter got into the car himself. Turning toward Beca, he informed her that because they had a distance to go before eating, their first stop would be a coffee shop for cappuccinos. As she was putting on her seatbelt she simply replied, "All right, let's get going." She ordered a raspberry latte while Peter got himself a French vanilla cappuccino from the coffee house.

While sipping slowly from the hot beverages they got on the expressway in the early November evening. Beca pried Peter for a hint as to their destination, but he just smiled at her attempts, stating, "You will see in time. Relax and enjoy your latte."

They talked about camping, biking, their yards, and the landscaping they had done, and what they were looking forward to doing in the future. It was the love of being outdoors that seemed to be a connecting factor in the relationship. The conversation continued into the area of jobs, with Beca bragging she really enjoyed her work environment and the people she worked with. Peter mentioned that for the most part he worked alone, building cabinets or placing trim in residential homes.

He turned off the expressway and headed toward the Michigan lakeshore. Coming into a small town, Peter expressed how he enjoyed the water and all the things associated with it. "Do you know what I'm talking about?" he asked Beca. "The sounds, the smells, well most of the smells." He laughed before adding, "There just seems to be a calming effect water has on ones mind and soul.

"Here we are!" Peter exclaimed, driving into the parking lot of a restaurant along the channel coming in from the big lake. Beca turned toward him and asked, "So this is it, the special place?"

"Oh yeah," he replied. "They have the best sea food menu in the northern hemisphere, and nobody goes hungry with their generous portions." Peter found a parking place and walked around the car, opening Beca's door before escorting her into the restaurant.

They were able to be seated immediately and each scanned their menu, pointing out interesting choices to the other. After placing the order with their drinks already before them, Peter pointed out the wonderful view from the dining area out over the channel. He stated that it was good this time of year due to the lack of crowds. "If you are not in a hurry and are willing to deal with all the people, the popular summer time has a much better view when it is full of boats and people."

The salads arrived, and just like last time, Peter hesitated and said "Excuse me," bowing his head in prayer, giving thanks for the meal before him. Beca felt the pressure and also bowed in a prayer of thanksgiving. When Peter raised his head, he noticed she also had bowed in prayer. When she finished, he commented, "Something I wanted to find out about you, Beca Stone, was if you are a religious person and what your true priorities and beliefs are. I need to be up front with you. I am looking for a wife, one who has a personal relationship with God. If you do not have or desire to have that, then this courtship should no longer continue."

Beca wasn't ready for this topic, but she could tell Peter was sincere. She put the dressing on her salad as she replied, "I did ask for time alone so we could talk in depth of who we are, didn't I?" She relayed how she attended—at least for the most part—the Bible church she had been brought up in, but also confessed she didn't spend time with God like her parents did. "Most people would call me a religious person because of my attendance at church," she told Peter.

Peter had been slowly eating his salad while listening intently to her. At her hesitation in the explanation, he stopped eating and informed her that he faithfully attended Faith Community Church. "I think the beliefs are comparable with Bible church teachings, if that's what you truly believe, Beca." He briefly held eye contact to drive his comment home. She felt slightly uncomfortable with his last comment, especially the way he looked at her while making it.

She looked questionably at Peter and asked, "What do you mean?"

He simply stated, "Whatever you believe, you will live. Religion is not a relationship; I believe a relationship requires involvement just like we are spending time together now." He continued, "I totally believe that if a couple cannot agree on their basic beliefs, they will have continuing conflicts in their marriage. Your beliefs are the core or base for all other decisions." Peter could see Beca was thinking deeply and felt he had gone far enough for the moment, so he suggested she start in on the salad before the meal came.

After they had finished the meal, Peter stated the next thing he had planned for the evening was a walk on the boardwalk. He commented, "I wish we could have done this when the weather was in our favor." Darkness had already set in by the time they started walking, but the walkway was lit.

Beca laughed as she found gloves in her coat pocket and put them on. "Nobody else is brave enough to be out here in November."

Peter smiled at her as he reached over taking her gloved hand in his, saying, "I better do my part keeping your hand warm too."

She smiled and her spirits soared when she felt his strong hand grasp hers.

Walking on the mostly abandoned boardwalk along the channel in the evening air was chilly but bearable. Peter and Beca conversed but continued to watch the walkway in the dim light. She admitted the tranquility along the water was therapeutic and could see why he liked the area. She asked, "Have you come here often?" He stated that he and his late wife Linda loved to spend time here, coming as often as they could, usually in the summer.

There were a few shops along the waterfront, but most were closed for the season. They found one still open because it also had access from the street side, so they slipped inside to dispel the chill for a few minutes. They browsed, making comments about some of the interesting, not to be found elsewhere items the waterfront tourist town shop had. Warmed, they exited the store, retracing their steps back toward the restaurant where the car was parked, again walking hand in hand.

Back in the car, Peter turned the heater on, removing any chill that remained from the evening walk as they started driving slowly down the street along the waterfront. Peter pointed out things that might be of interest to Beca during the normal season, even if the darkness prevented seeing it. Leaving the waterfront, he continued giving her a tour of the quaint town, including some of its history, before they headed out of town.

"Where are we going?" Beca asked in an alarming manner. "Isn't the expressway in the other direction?"

Peter glanced over at her and lightly caressed her hand that was resting on the console and asked, "Didn't you want to spend time alone getting to know each other?" He immediately followed with, "Relax. I'm sorry if I put you on the defensive. I just wanted to show you where I grew up. It's just a couple of miles out of town."

Breathing a sigh of relief, Beca commented, "Now I understand why you like this town and seem to know so much about it.

It's nice you wanted to surprise me but," then she added harshly, "I would really appreciate it in the future if you were a little more up front in certain situations."

Peter apologized and indicated he had not thought about how she might perceive his intentions.

Slowing down, Peter pointed at a dimly lit farmhouse and simply said, "That's where I spent the first twenty-one years of my life."

Beca questioned him, "Did you intend to stop and introduce me to your parents?"

He quickly replied, "I certainly would not assume you were ready for that without discussing it with you." He continued driving past the house. "Besides, my parents moved shortly after I got married, so the people living there now might be shocked if I introduced you."

Beca laughed and agreed it might be rather awkward, then she asked Peter where his parents currently resided.

"They bought a condo in town," he stated. "My dad was tired of the upkeep, and Mom wanted to be closer to things. My original intention was to drive by their condo as the last point of interest before heading back home, if that's all right with you." He looked at her inquisitively waiting for confirmation.

She smiled in approval and replied, "I would like that, and I sure don't want to ruin your well-thought-out, get-to-know-who-you-are evening."

This time it was Peter who laughed.

During the lengthy ride back to Beca's house, Peter—who was still trying to determine the future of their relationship—brought the subject of God up again. "Beca," he inquired, "pertaining to the earlier conversation of your belief in God, I am serious about knowing where you stand to determine if we should continue this courtship."

Beca answered cautiously because she wanted to continue seeing him, but she knew she needed to be honest with both him and herself. "As a young girl I did commit my life to God," she said, "but if I'm honest with myself and you, it hasn't gone much further than my attending church on a pretty regular basis. I guess I don't spend time with God or on the relationship like I should."

He looked longingly at her before he replied, "I appreciate your honesty." He sat momentarily pondering what she had just revealed to him. Beca had no more to say on the subject at this time, so she sat silently. Finally Peter stole a glance over at her and said, "I'm willing to continue this relationship. However, I can't express how important the issue of a solid relationship with God is."

Finally back at Beca's home, the hour was already late. Peter shut the car off and just sat there looking at her. She looked back while searching his eyes before commenting, "You are slightly mysterious, Peter Bell, but I still want to thank you for the interesting evening. I enjoyed it very much." Then she asked, in a slow drawn out manner, "So, are you going to walk me to the door?"

Peter took a deep breath and referred to the comment just made, "So you think I'm mysterious? Well let me be perfectly clear so there is no misunderstanding, young lady."

Beca was slightly shocked by his demeanor but was enticed at the same time. He continued, "Last time we were together, we parted with a hug. Suddenly I feel ready for a first kiss." He sat on pins and needles waiting for a reply while searching her eyes, somehow hoping she felt the same way.

Time stood still for a brief moment. She had not expected him to be so forward. Then silently she slowly leaned over the console toward him allowing him that first kiss. It did not last long, and neither spoke as Peter exited the vehicle.

He made his way around the car to open the door for her. As she walked the few steps to the door, she heard Peter shut her car door. She thought he was right behind her as she unlocked the door to her house. Turning, she saw Peter getting back in the car. He waved as he backed out of the drive, leaving her standing alone with her thoughts.

DECISIONS

Soon after getting home from her date with Peter, Beca realized just how tired she was and quickly retired for the evening. She had mixed emotions from the events of the day but was just too tired to deal with any of them right now.

Lisa was not at church Sunday, frustrating Beca who needed a close friend to talk to. When her mother came over to say "hi" after the service, she determined not to mention anything of the previous evening. Elaine Stone greeted her daughter with a cheerful "it's nice to see you today," then complimented her outfit. Beca indulged in the small talk, anticipating an undesired question from her mother. "Oh yeah," her mother injected as they were concluding, Beca braced herself thinking *here it comes.* "We are going to your brother Jake's house for Thanksgiving. I told him it would be nice to ask you too, so he gave me permission to invite you, hopefully you don't have any plans yet."

She was relieved and did not hesitate with a reply. "I have no plans and appreciate the invite, so tell Jake and Kris to figure on it. Maybe we can ride together," she suggested to her mother. "We can work out the details later."

Once home, Beca prepared herself a lunch of soup with a tossed salad. As she sat alone by the kitchen table, she really wanted to talk to someone and thought of her friend Rhonda. She had previously shared some of her soap opera life with her, so she decided to give her a call. She relayed to Rhonda how she really could use a listening friend at the moment, indicating it had to do with her dating life. Rhonda told her to put the coffee on; she was coming right over because this was face-to-face kind of stuff.

Beca was grateful for friends who were nonjudgmental, trustworthy, caring, and confidential, she thought maybe curiosity drove them slightly too.

Rhonda brought over a pound cake to go with the coffee, stating you can't have coffee without having something to wash down. The two longtime friends took up residence in Beca's living room with cake and coffee. Once settled in Rhonda pushed her friend to spill the beans.

This time she opened up to Rhonda, telling how she liked both men, but now they both wanted deeper relationships and neither one knew about the other. She felt she was not being upfront with either one of them and was starting to be concerned about making a mistake, possibly losing the one she wanted to keep, or even losing both of them when they discovered her little game.

She continued, "Right now I'm confused; I don't know what I want. I just don't want to make a decision I might regret later.

Rhonda slowly sipped her coffee, washing down another bite of pound cake before she spoke. "Beca, Beca, Beca," Rhonda gave no hint as to her direction, keeping her in suspense. "Part of me envies you, and part is glad I'm on the outside looking in.

The real question is what do *you* want? Not what does everybody else want."

Beca confided, "I'm not sure anymore. I'm actually content alone, but then there were times I wish I had someone to share life with. Now I have the opportunity to choose, and I don't want to blow it."

Silence fell for a few moments before Rhonda spoke boldly. "The first thing you need to do is make the decision whether you want to be single or pursue someone to share life with. Make that decision then stick to it. I think you already know the answer but are afraid of losing control or failing for fear of the unknown. So, what's it gonna be?"

Beca was aghast at the harsh tone her friend had taken, especially in her own house! They had been friends a long time; this was not how she imagined the girl talk proceeding. She held her tongue long enough for her mind to convict her that Rhonda was right. But why was it so hard to admit?

Finally Beca spoke exactly what was on her mind, "Rhonda that was harsh! You actually were beginning to make me mad, and as much as I hate to, I must admit you're right. I do know what I want; it's to share my life with someone special—like you and Roger, or Jillian and Chad. I want someone to love, cherish, and make memories with, someone to say "good night" to." Having voiced her true desires she sighed and exclaimed, "Wow! That's a relief. I guess I've only been fooling myself!"

Rhonda, feeling slightly guilty for hitting her so hard, humbly asked, "So, is our friendship still good?"

Beca abruptly laughed at both Rhonda's question and the new tone she had taken then answered, "We're good."

Beca felt rejuvenated with the admission, so she once again pried Rhonda for information, hoping for further direction. "I think we just drew a conclusion to the first issue you had mentioned, so now what?" she asked.

Rhonda saw she was serious, so she agreed to make one more comment. "Beca," she said, waiting for her friend to give undivided attention, "I know we differ slightly in our religious beliefs as friends, but my husband and I have the same convictions, so if there is one piece of quality counsel I can give you, it's this: the strongest marriage is both husband and wife being on the same page in your religious beliefs. So, whether it's Peter or Jason, have the same beliefs because that's what you base all your decisions on."

Beca smiled as she remembered someone else had told her basically the same thing recently. Now she knew for sure what she needed to find out and also sort out in her own life. She nodded in agreement at the insight, thanking her for the words of wisdom.

Rhonda noted the slipping time and hastily said "good-bye" as she retreated to her car.

As Beca was cleaning the remaining dishes from her lunch the doorbell rang. She walked to the door, wondering who had come to visit her late on a Sunday afternoon. Standing unexpectedly at her door was Jason, holding a single yellow rose. She opened the door and expressed her surprise. Seeing the flower, she asked, "Is that flower for me?"

Jason immediately started rambling about how he knew the visit was a surprise, but he had hoped she was home. She invited him into the entryway, stating it was a bit chilly out. After stepping inside, he explained how they told him at work on Friday the parent company was sending him to school for a week. It was some new computer class to learn how to inventory with a new database. Then he stopped mid sentence and handed her the rose saying, "I'm sorry, I'm just babbling on. This is for my stand-alone beauty queen."

Beca was flattered, but also a bit perturbed. Jason had not called ahead, assuming their relationship had progressed this far. However, she still invited him into the house with a disclaimer it was not prepared for guests, and that she was just cleaning up the kitchen.

Inside he noticed the two coffee cups and two plates that she had not washed yet, so he questioned her why two cups and plates. Did she need two or did she have some company earlier?

Now Beca wondered if he suspected another man in her life, but saw no harm in answering him truthfully. She told Jason she had her friend Rhonda over for coffee and pound cake, so they could have some girl talk. He seemed satisfied as he changed the subject back to his work issue.

"Beca," he started, "I just had to see you because I'm leaving for Chicago, early tomorrow morning and don't come back until next Friday evening. I'm sorry for the intrusion, but I was hoping the rose covered my sporadic behavior."

She summed up the current dilemma before concluding there was no harm done, and besides, she did have the evening open. She told him to find a seat in the living room while she made another pot of coffee.

Remembering Jason was allergic to cats, Beca shooed Missy into the bedroom. Talking loudly from the living room, Jason commented on the homey feeling the room gave with the pastel colors and the mini wagon by the fireplace.

"Thanks," Beca replied in his direction and asked if he wanted some of the leftover pound cake with his coffee.

Jason let her know he was impressed how tidy she kept her house as she served him the coffee and pound cake. She sat down with only a cup of coffee commenting, "I've had enough cake for today." She asked about the schooling and why they chose him to go.

He replied, "I guess they think single guys have no life."

It's ironic, thought Beca as she remembered her conversation with Rhonda over the last couple of hours. Jason, the one she needed to talk to showed up at her doorstep. She certainly had not anticipated having any serious talks so soon. For lack of issues to discuss and having one that seemed a priority, she convinced herself to at least bring the subject up so it was out there.

She was nervous and felt extremely warm as she started to address Jason. She had to push herself to keep from chickening out. "Jason," she began, "we've had a few dates and have gotten to know each other somewhat, and I for one enjoy being with you, and hopefully you feel the same about me." She hesitated momentarily as she watched Jason who started breaking into a broad smile; he seemed to enjoy the direction of the conversation. "There is one serious topic we have not touched on," she boldly continued. She noticed the smile leave his face. Jason was now looking at her in a quizzical manner. *Don't stop now*, she told herself, *it will be harder later and you are already into it*, so she continued. "It's of the religious nature," she blurted, almost embarrassed at her forwardness. "We have never talked about our beliefs, and I think it's rather important if we are to continue this relationship."

Jason's smile came back, relieving her anxiety as he replied, "You are absolutely correct; it is a major issue for any relationship, and we do need to talk about it. I apologize for not being the one to bring it up."

All of a sudden Missy came running into the room; she jumped on Beca's lap, causing her to spill some of the remaining coffee. Beca got up saying "excuse me a minute." She grabbed Missy, scolding her while carrying the cat back to the bedroom, asking, "How did you get out?"

She brought a few paper towels into the living room to wipe herself up, along with the small mess the spill had created. She apologized to Jason for the cat's behavior and for her new customized look.

He laughed and informed her, "I guess I never told you, but I have a dog, so I'm used to the interruptions for attention purposes. He's a boxer, and his name is Buddy." The intrusion over, Jason turned the conversation back to their previous topic.

"My parents took me to church when I was young," Jason stated, "but I only go once in a while, mostly to appease them. Plus it makes me feel good at the same time. In my own mind I believe church is a good thing, but it has never been a priority for me."

"So, what denomination do you attend when you do go?" Beca asked.

Jason stated, "It was community church rather fundamental; it's called Faith Community. Instantly a red flag arose as she remembered Peter had stated he attended a Faith Community. *Could it be the same church?* she wondered. Maybe these two men knew each other. Searching for additional information, she asked, "So how big is the church and how often do you attend?"

"Well," Jason slowly replied as if trying to recall something from a long time ago, "my best guess is maybe about six hundred people, and I attend probably an average of once a month."

It didn't take long for Beca to figure out that if they did both go to the same church with only six hundred people, they more than likely at least knew who the other was. She had to find out, so she asked Jason one more question. "So where is the church located?"

Again he momentarily searched his mind before replying, "I don't know the name of the street; it's just off M37, by the old airport. Do you know where I'm talking about?"

Beca nodded her head in acknowledging that she did. Then she tried changing the subject, asking Jason if he wanted more coffee or pound cake. He patted his stomach while stating, "There is no more room here. Besides, I need to get home to Buddy. I really am sorry for the way I intruded this afternoon, but I just had to see you before going off to school this week."

Beca followed him to the door, where he stopped and leaned toward her, expecting a kiss good-bye. She held back, allowing him to kiss her only on the cheek while saying, "Have a good week at school. Call me when you get back."

After Jason left, Beca released Missy from her prison then slipped into her pajamas before making a bowl of popcorn. She retreated to the living room and flipped the television on. Slumping into her favorite chair with her legs curled up under her, she decided to relax the remainder of the evening.

The television was on, but Beca wasn't watching it. Her thoughts were dominated by what had taken place that day. She told herself it was a good thing she had not gone to church with either one of them, although she still needed to confirm it was the same church. She certainly couldn't ask if they knew each other. "Is the world that small?" she asked out loud. *Well, at least I'm compatible with both of them in my beliefs,* she reasoned. *Although it might have been easier if I had been compatible with only one of them.*

As she tried to sort things out, she determined she really did need her friends' input and support. Rhonda's pushiness had helped her find information that could have been devastating if revealed in the wrong fashion. Lisa also had helped by convincing her to give it time and let it work itself out.

Beca knew Jason was gone for the week, and she had just had a date with Peter, so she felt no immediate pressure to make any rash decisions. She did know decisions had to be made and that the longer she waited, the more difficult it would become.

Maybe, she schemed, *I can use the excuse of the upcoming Thanksgiving holiday and busyness of the Christmas season to stretch things out or slow them down, allowing time to work out my priorities.* "I'm still in control," Beca boldly stated out loud, although she was not totally convinced of it.

Monday evening Beca could stand it no longer; she needed a sounding board, so she called her friend Rhonda, who presently happened to be the most up to date on her personal saga. Roger, Rhonda's husband, answered and informed her that his wife had gone out for the evening and was not due back until late, so she called Lisa instead. She needed someone to talk to now. Her mind had been driving her crazy with thoughts of the two men in her life, not sure how all this was going to play out.

Lisa said she was available to talk, but only as long as her kids behaved because her husband was gone for the evening. Beca held nothing back as her emotions kicked in. She knew Lisa was an understanding confidant and good listener, so she brought her up to date, including the previous night's surprise visit from Jason. When she finished, she suggested Lisa tell her the truth just give it straight.

Just then she heard a crash in the background, and a child started crying. Lisa quickly said, "I'm sorry, Beca. I'll have to call you back; I have a situation to deal with right now." Lisa immediately hung up, leaving a stunned Beca holding onto her phone with a dial tone in her ear.

The agony of waiting for a return call was nothing less than torture for her. She had said her piece without any comment or reaction from Lisa. As sensitive as the relational situation was becoming, she decided to get Rhonda's input too. She reasoned she could make wiser decisions with more counsel. Besides,

Rhonda was already involved. Beca hoped—with the input of her friends—she could make the right decision about her future.

Finally, Lisa called back after what seemed like hours in Beca's mind, but in reality was only about fifteen minutes. Lisa gave her grave analysis as she listened quietly. "Beca," she started, "I told you it could get sticky. If I hear you correctly, you feel one of these two men is Mr. Right for you, but you're not sure which one yet, right?"

Beca gave her a one-word answer. "Yes."

"All right, I will make one suggestion, for whatever it's worth. Take a sheet of paper and make a side-by-side comparison list of each man's good and bad points, along with their goals and dreams. Then make a list of yourself with the same criteria, compare the lists for compatibility. I do have one warning for you, and I don't want you to take it lightly." Lisa raised her voice slightly to drive the point home. "When you make the list on yourself, be honest as to what your desires and dreams are, not what others expect or things that you feel safe with."

Beca had expected Lisa to say it would all work out. Now she was spellbound, thinking of the assignment she had given her. She thanked Lisa for the input and assured her she would give it a try.

Tuesday evening, Beca finished the dishes before sitting down to start the lists Lisa had suggested. In the beginning it was easy filling the sheets in on Peter and Jason; the hard part was their desires and dreams. She had not spent much time talking about future goals with either one of them. She began to realize just how wise Lisa was in assigning the task, causing her to think beyond the present.

The doorbell rang, and she jumped at the unexpected noise. Standing at the door were both Rhonda and Jillian. Beca, bewildered, said, "Come on in." She quickly hid the lists she had been working on.

Rhonda spoke first, "Hey, Beca, Roger told me about your phone call last night, and I just knew you needed a couple of friends to talk to. Sorry we didn't call first, we thought we'd surprise you. I hope you're not mad at me, but I kinda caught Jillian up on the guy stuff on our way here."

Beca bit her lip. She was thankful and ticked at the same time, knowing her friends cared but wondered what else was going on behind her back.

The friends each took a seat in the living room. Initially nobody spoke as Jillian and Rhonda just sat waiting for Beca to take the lead. She was trying to put her thoughts together, wondering if her friends were ganging up or actually trying to help.

Finally Beca broke the silence. "How much did Rhonda tell you, Jillian?"

"I guess most of what she knew, like how confusing things have gotten for you and how you need some understanding friends to lean on," Jillian answered.

Turning to face Rhonda, Beca smiled slightly before speaking. "There have been some new developments since we talked."

Rhonda's mouth dropped open as she exclaimed, "Girl, we just can't keep up with you. Now what?"

"Jason stopped over after we talked on Sunday. We spent some time talking," she explained excitedly. "We talked briefly about religious things, like you suggested we needed to, and guess what!" Beca was on the edge of her chair with excitement written all over her face. Both Rhonda and Jillian asked "what" at the same time, with the same enthusiasm she was displaying.

"I'm not one hundred percent sure," she exploded, "but I think Peter and Jason attend the same church! I'm glad I found that out before anything got serious," she blurted in an excited tone of voice. Then Beca sat back in her chair while her friends digested this latest development. She waited briefly before throwing out her next question, "Now what?"

Jillian said the first thing that came to her mind, "Girl, you are in so much trouble!"

Beca shot back, "That's why I have friends! Help?"

They all laughed at the pathetic plea, even Beca. "All right," said Rhonda. "Let's all keep cool, it can still be worked out."

Rhonda spoke first, asking a few questions. "Do you know both men well enough to make a decision as to which one? Is time still on your side? Are you ready for all this? How can we help?"

Beca sighed deeply as she answered Rhonda with, "I don't know. I'm confused, that's too many questions at one time."

Jillian spoke softly to ease the tension placed on Beca, stating, "Soon you need to make a choice. You can't lead both men on for very long, it's not fair to them or you." Then she gave demanding insight by boldly saying, "Stop trying to figure the guys out and figure out who Beca Stone is first. Only then will the other decisions come easy." Rhonda nodded in agreement, saying, "I absolutely agree."

Beca had no reply as she contemplated the words Jillian had spoken in love.

As the two friends left they both gave Beca a big hug, telling her they loved her but could not and would not make her decisions for her. "Good luck!" Rhonda shouted as they left her standing in the doorway.

After they left she did not go back to her lists but spent time thoughtfully reviewing the last couple of weeks. She finally drew the conclusion it was her religious beliefs and practices dictating who she was.

Thanksgiving was only two weeks away, and Beca had no dates this weekend, giving her a brief reprieve. With all the sharing she had done by looking for direction through her friends, she realized she had not allowed her parents a chance to give input. She came up with excuses and reasons to keep it that way, but in the end, she knew they only wanted to help her. She called them, asking if they were available to talk on Saturday morning. Josh Stone suggested they meet her at a local restaurant for breakfast at eight. Beca quickly agreed, reminding him to bring Mom.

Saturday morning as Beca backed her car out of the garage, she noticed the thermometer inside the car told her it was only thirty degrees outside. "I guess my bike riding is done for the year," she spoke at the gage. "It's just too cold now."

At the restaurant Beca was walking in as her parents drove into the parking lot, so she gave the hostess a heads up for three people. They were seated immediately and each ordered the bottomless cup of coffee to start. She asked about her parents' health and how their week had gone. The waitress returned with the coffee and asked for their breakfast orders. After orders were placed and the coffee sampled, Beca leaned forward indicating she had something important to say.

I know Thanksgiving is coming soon and we will all be together at Jake's house, but I wanted to talk to just the two of you in private. I don't want you hearing things through the grapevine about my personal life. I still need to work a few things out, and maybe you can give me some encouragement or wisdom from your years of experience. So, that being said, please let me tell the whole story before any comments. Okay?" She raised her eyebrows and looked hard at her mother while waiting for confirmation.

"Yes, dear," her mother responded as she glanced over at her husband, who was sipping his coffee as if nothing had been said.

"Here it is," she began. I told you I've been dating two men at the same time, each has his own set of qualities that I am drawn to. However we all know eventually it comes down to choosing one—or at least one at a time—to have a deeper relationship. Presently I am still uncertain and feel I may need a little more time with each of them to know which one is right for me. Yes, Mom, I know what I'm getting myself into, especially when I found out they may even attend the same church."

Her mother showed alarm but expressed nothing verbally, sticking to the request Beca made to let her tell the whole story first.

"I came to the conclusion just this week that I need to know about myself first. Like what my goals and dreams are, before I can make a decision pertaining to either Peter or Jason." Beca noticed her mother itching to say something, so she held up her finger in a just one minute fashion, holding her off as she continued. "There is one other thing that has come to my attention recently." She stopped abruptly while trying to put her thoughts into proper words, knowing no matter how she said it, her parents would have a reaction. "I need to figure out my relationship with God," Beca stated, because that's what people base their decisions on—it's their guidelines for life.

"I'm done now," she said, sitting back in her seat while waiting for her parents' reaction. None came as both her parents smiled and shook their heads in agreement with what she had just told them. This bothered her more than if they gave her an earful, so she tried to ignite feedback by asking, "Don't either one of you have anything to say?"

"Honey," her mom replied, "what you just told us is what we always wanted to hear from you, so there is nothing more we can say. We are so proud of you, and as your father told you before, you're an adult with good judgment who can make her own decisions." Then she forcefully added, "So let's eat and enjoy each other's company."

Beca was slightly bewildered by the way the conversation had gone, but she was content knowing that her parents trusted her and didn't try to run her life. She thanked them for listening, and they in return, thanked her for allowing them to share in her personal life.

After the breakfast with her parents, she did some shopping, before heading home to do the housework that she had been neglecting, because for the past few days she just didn't feel like it. As Beca was completing her household cleaning tasks, she looked at the clock only to realize she had missed lunch. She still was not that hungry after the larger than normal breakfast she had at the restaurant that morning, but told herself she needed to eat anyway, especially after exerting all the energy by cleaning that morning.

Shopping, cleaning, and lunch done, Beca questioned, *Now what am I going to do the rest of the day?* She remembered the comparison list Lisa had prompted her to make, aiding her in decision-making. With the cool overcast day, she decided it was a good time for a warm, cozy fire, so she brought some wood in and lit the fire. Before sitting down she made herself a cup of hot chocolate then settled into that favorite old chair of hers with the comparison lists she had already started.

The sounds and sight of the crackling fire, the smells from the cherry and oak wood, plus the added warmth it provided, along with the taste of the hot chocolate excited all Beca's senses at the same time, giving her a feeling of momentary utopia. She wished she could hold the feeling indefinitely as she took out the list, picking up where she had left off.

With list complete for the two men, she noticed a pattern that intrigued her. She had filled out the lists as complete as possible with what she knew about each man. Then she completed a list on herself as she finished the cup of now warm chocolate. The fire was in need of attention, so she got up to attend it, almost stepping on Missy who had curled up at the base of her chair. She added wood to the fire, breathing deeply, enjoying the scent it produced.

Beca noticed the house still smelled of Saturday's fire when she was preparing to go to church the next morning. She wondered if anyone in church might be able to smell it also, so she applied extra perfume, hoping to at least overpower it.

At church the usual friends and family conversed, but there was no mention—at least not to her—about the smell of fire. The sermon topic was about how each one of us will some day give an account for ourselves before the Lord, and it made Beca squirm slightly because she felt it was meant for her. She was a believer, but she knew her life didn't always reflect it.

After church her mother came over to remind her Thursday was Thanksgiving, then indicated they expected her to ride with them to Jake's house. "We are leaving at nine thirty sharp, and please bring a salad," she stated while walking away, giving Beca no chance for argument.

Sunday afternoon Beca had dozed off while reading, before the phone jarred her awake. It was Peter, asking if she had plans for Thanksgiving and if not, maybe she could accompany him to his parents' home and meet them. She softly answered Peter by saying, "I'm sorry, I will be spending the holiday at my brother's house with my parents."

She could hear the disappointment in his voice when he replied, "That's nice. I hope you enjoy your time together."

"Thanks," she said. "I have the rest of the week off, maybe your folks will have some leftovers they need help with."

Peter was both surprised and impressed by her candor "They probably will have." Thinking quickly, he asked, "Will you accompany Ruth and I to church Sunday? Then we could go to my parents' house afterward and help them clean up those leftovers."

That was not what Beca had expected; now she was in an awkward position. She ho-hummed a bit before admitting she wasn't sure about the church thing. Peter explained, "It works best for time if we attend church with my parents in the morning before lunch."

Relieved it was not Faith Community, where she might run into Jason, she agreed to accompany him, trying hard to make him believe it was a difficult decision.

"We will pick you up next Sunday morning at eight thirty," he said, promising her another latte on the way before he hung up.

Monday evening Jason called as Beca expected he might after being out of town the previous week. She knew both relationships were starting to be more than just friends, and the time was drawing short for her to come clean. Both men were still in the dark concerning the other. She knew when this came to light, they might feel betrayed or even think she had been using them.

Jason, as expected, asked her for another evening of time together. They made arrangements for the upcoming Saturday, with Jason picking her up at five o'clock, allowing them plenty of time together. Jason informed her he wanted to take her to a fancy place this time, asking her to dress accordingly.

LETTING GO

Beca was actually wishing she had not gotten herself involved with two men at the same time. She liked them both but for different reasons. So far she had been fortunate enough to keep things straight, but she felt her luck was running out quickly, so she agonizingly gave herself a deadline of two weeks to end one of the relationships.

Once again work was busy for her because contractors were trying to squeeze projects in before the Thanksgiving holiday. Business kept her from thinking about personal issues during the day, but the nights seemed long as she reviewed her lists and focused on her own goals and dreams for the future. When quitting time finally arrived Wednesday, Beca was in good spirits as she looked forward to family time and the two planned dates. She kept herself busy Wednesday evening by making the salad for Thursday's dinner. Then she watched movies until her eyes wouldn't stay open.

Thanksgiving morning brought a light dusting of snow, the first of the season actually. Beca carefully ventured onto the slightly slippery road, mentally switching to her winter driving habits as she headed over to her parents' house. The ride to Jake's home with her parents was uneventful and quiet, but once there activity and conversations thrived, especially with the three boys, who seemed overjoyed to have the whole family together.

During the feast it was nonstop talking until Jake nonchalantly asked, "So, Beca anything new on the man front we need to be updated on?"

Only Robert, Jake and Kris's three-year-old was still jabbering, the rest of the table fell dead silent. Beca dealt with the question calmly by replying, "Sorry to disappoint you little brother, but I have nothing to report at this time."

Later as she was helping Kris with the dishes, Kris again asked her if there was anything on the guy front.

This time with just the two girls in the kitchen, she told her sister-in-law she had been dating two guys who didn't know about each other, and now they were both becoming more than friends. "I know it can't continue," she stated. "I like them both too, that's why it's frustrating me so much." Then she told Kris as tears welled up in her eyes showing her emotions, "I'm going to call it quits with one of them in a week or two." Then she added, "This relationship stuff is so hard!"

On the return trip to her parents' house, Beca convinced her mother they needed to go antique shopping on Friday, mostly for something to do rather than just sitting around being bored.

Friday slipped by quickly as mother and daughter hit numerous antique shops with a side trip to a café for lunch. The air was crisp but dry all day, adding seasonal ambience to the pleasure trip. Apparently there were other people who had the same idea of filling their Friday with shopping. The shops were busy, with the upcoming Christmas season, but it also added to the cheery atmosphere.

During this shopping trip, Beca purchased only a jewelry box while her mother bought a ring. Beca made the comment to her mother that if she needed a place to store the ring, she had a jewelry box to keep it in. Both laughed as her mother replied, "Try to get it."

Before parting ways she informed her mother not to expect her in church because she was attending another church with Peter Sunday morning.

Her mother responded without any expression, "I see."

Saturday Beca woke feeling nervous about the date with Jason that evening. Tonight was time with Jason, and tomorrow was time with Peter. Did she really need another week to make a decision when she already knew the answer? Maybe out of courtesy she was giving someone a last chance to win her over, but then again she was leading him on, and he didn't even know it.

She wondered out loud, "What kind of person am I? If I am honest with them, will they both ditch me? Can I just say it isn't working with the one and continue with the other keeping the truth to myself? How would they know?"

Around four o'clock she started getting ready for her date with Jason; she wanted it to be special. She showered before putting on the new dress she had purchased that morning. The dress was a deep blue with a white collar; its length was just below the knee, still revealing plenty of leg. She usually preferred not wearing much makeup or perfume, but tonight she applied a little extra, telling herself it was an attention getter. She also put a slight curl in her shoulder length light brown hair. Pleased with the outcome, she talked to the mirror saying, "Jason you poor boy, you won't know what hit ya."

Five o'clock on the nose Jason rang the doorbell. Beca grabbed a black jacket that she thought completed the ensemble, to keep her warm for the evening. As she opened the door to join Jason, he just stood there wide-eyed, so she smiled tenderly at him.

He held no emotion back as he exclaimed, "Wow, you look fantastic. I think I love you, Beca! You are absolutely positively the most beautiful woman I have ever known!"

Beca smiled before whispering a shy thank you then asked tenderly, "Can we go now?"

Jason was still standing in the way of her exiting the house. "Of course," he muttered as he stepped back to let her proceed, then he quickly made his way to open her car door. Still gazing at her in an awestruck manner, he closed the door behind her.

"Well, you sure do look handsome," Beca complemented Jason who was actually wearing a tie—she had never seen him this formal before and was impressed. She asked, "Where are we going tonight for such an upscale dinner?"

As Jason started the car and began backing out of the drive he replied, "You will see soon enough."

The ride ended twenty minutes later, when they pulled into the lot of a restaurant called Solos. Beca had heard of the place but had never darkened the door herself, probably because she had heard it was pricy.

She looked over at Jason and inquired, "Are you sure you want to eat here?"

He smiled as he sternly stated, "I want to make this night special for the person who makes me feel special. Nothing is too good for you, my dear." Then he got out of the car and made his way to her side to open the door for her.

Reservations had been made ahead of time, so they were escorted right in. Once seated, Jason again complemented Beca by saying he really liked the dress. He also noted she had put some curls in her hair, and he somehow thought it made her face glow. She wanted to hold onto the feeling of confidence and self worth Jason was giving her at that moment. All she could do was smile and whisper a gentle "thank you." Then she began to scan the menu before her on the table.

They talked and laughed throughout the lengthy five-course meal. She was surprised how quickly the time had slipped by when they finally exited the restaurant. It was still somewhat early but too late to do much else for the evening.

Jason had already planned ahead, informing her they were taking a moonlit ride. The ride ended at a boat launch by a small lake where Jason put the car in park. The moon cast a light glow across the water, and Beca thought she even saw a few snowflakes drifting down.

He turned toward her in a matter of fact way and stated, "I think it's time we talk about where our relationship is headed. I want you to know right up front"—then he stopped as he looked into her eyes through the darkness in the car, before completing his sentence—"I love you, Beca. I need to know if you feel the same way."

Great, she thought, *the night was going so well, why did he have to do this tonight?* This was rather unexpected, and he was waiting for an immediate answer. She sat there—intently searching his face—but did not speak for fear of saying something she might regret. It was quiet except for the sound of the engine and the fan from the heater keeping them warm.

Jason slowly dropped his gaze and hung his head before saying in a quivering voice, "So that's it, uh? You can't answer me, so I can only assume you do not feel the same way." He again raised his head to look at her.

She was still looking at him, and it melted her heart when she saw the tears welling up in his eyes.

"I do love you, Jason," she started, giving him false hope. "I'm just not sure we are right for each other."

He immediately interrupted her by proclaiming in a louder than expected voice, "If there is something about me I need to change, I will change for you, Beca!"

She sighed and hung her head, feeling disappointment in herself for letting the relationship get to this point. "I'm sorry, Jason. Maybe it could have worked if it had been another time in our lives. I just don't know what else to say. I'm sorry." She was torn, knowing she was still not telling Jason the whole truth.

He shifted in his seat, staring straight ahead for what seemed forever, then suddenly shifted the car into gear and began turning around to bring Beca home.

She lost the confidence and even self-worth she experienced earlier; guilt set in convicting her she had misled Jason. At the very least she owed him an explanation before she left the car. It might be her last opportunity to set things straight with him and her conscience.

Jason pulled into the drive and placed the car in park, but left the car running. He just sat there indicating to Beca he had no intention of coming to open her car door or escort her to the house.

She did not exit the vehicle as Jason had expected her to, but turned toward him while he stared straight ahead. "Jason," she began, with tears welling up in her eyes, "you are a wonderful man. I know there is nothing I can say at this point to smooth this over or comfort you. I hope you will forgive me, because I need to be honest with you, or I can't forgive myself."

He looked up at her in a puzzled manner, but she quickly looked away before speaking. In a broken voice, she bluntly stated, "I have been dating someone else." Looking back at Jason with a face full of expression to show the compassion she felt, she continued. "I know it was not right or fair to you. I'm so sorry, I'm so sorry." She could no longer hold back the tears. Not knowing what else to do at this point, she opened the car door and got out, leaving Jason sitting there alone.

Once inside the house, she continued sobbing as the bottled up emotions escaped. She had never experienced disappointing somebody she cared about before. After a couple of minutes, she peered outside to see if Jason had left. She saw the drive was as vacant and empty as she now felt.

Making herself a cup of hot chocolate was the best therapy she could muster, under the circumstances. She had not expected the night to end this way. She knew sleep would not come easy tonight, so she plopped down in her chair, sipping the hot chocolate. She turned on the television to help occupy her mind.

With the hot chocolate long gone and not much more than infomercials on the television in the early morning hours, Beca made her way to the bedroom to see if she could fall asleep.

FAMILY TIES

Was that the doorbell? Beca thought she was imagining the sound as she woke up to the bright sunshine poking through the blinds in her room. It rang again, and she sprang out of the bed, took one look at the clock to see it read eight twenty-eight, and she groaned, suddenly remembering her commitment to spend Sunday with Peter. She threw on a robe before making a quick stop in the bathroom. She tried to make herself somewhat presentable before answering the door.

Opening the door but trying to hide behind it, she informed Peter she had overslept and needed time to get ready. Apologizing, she invited him to bring Ruth inside while they waited for her. She took her clothes into the bathroom and in record time took a shower, blew her hair dry, brushed her teeth, applied makeup, and added perfume and even some jewelry before emerging. As she turned toward the bedroom, she stopped long enough to shout to Peter who was waiting patiently in the living room with Ruth, "I just need to get my shoes on and will be right out, if you want to get Ruth back in her car seat.

Beca had slipped on her black jacket, grabbed her Bible and made it to Peter's car just as he completed buckling Ruth in. He made a quick move to open the car door for her, while she breathlessly said "thank you" and settled into the passenger's seat. Suddenly it dawned on her, in her haste she had put on the same blue dress she had worn for the date with Jason the night before, but there was no going back now.

Peter was backing out of the drive while Beca expressed how sorry she was for the inconvenience she created by oversleeping. She explained she had a rough time getting to sleep last night and on top of that, forgot to set the alarm. Peter commended her for the speedy recovery, indicating they still had time for the latte he had promised her on the way if she still wanted it. She readily accepted the offer, stating, "If ever I needed one of those, it's today."

During the ride to church, Peter told Beca he liked the dress she was wearing and that she looked exceptionally nice. He also said he was looking forward to introducing her to his parents as he gently reached over to hold her hand.

Having gathered her composure after the latte and the lengthy ride to Peter's hometown, Beca looked forward to what the day held. Ruth had been much more subdued compared to the last time they spent time together, so Beca inquired of Peter if she felt well.

"She's fine," Peter spoke softly. "I had a talk with her before we picked you up so she wouldn't talk your ear off."

Beca smiled and thought, *she listens quite well for a four-year-old*, before commenting back, "I really don't mind, as a matter of fact I like talking to her."

Having heard the adults, Ruth asked, "Can I talk more now, Daddy?"

Beca laughed at her inquiry.

Peter answered, "After church, honey." They were just turning into the church parking lot.

"You didn't tell me it was a Bible church your parents attended," Beca quietly reprimanded Peter.

He smiled, slightly asking, "Does it matter?"

"Well, yeah," she replied. "It helps to know how you were raised."

As Peter parked the car he made the comment, "I can only open the door for one of you girls."

Ruth excitedly shouted, "Me, Daddy, me! Let me out!"

Beca laughed as he answered, "All right. I'll open the door for both of you."

Inside the church Beca felt out of place, knowing only Peter and his daughter. She was glad it was a small church. A couple approached them as Ruth exclaimed, "Nana! Papa!"

Here goes, she thought, *the introduction to the parents.* Peter introduced his parents as Tom and Cindy Bell then turned and said, "Mom, Dad, this is the wonderful lady I've been telling you about. I'd like you to meet Beca Stone."

The introduction was kept short due to the service starting in just a few minutes, so they ventured into the sanctuary and occupied a row together.

After the service Peter introduced Beca to a few other people, those who knew him from having grown up in the church. At the condo she inquired if she could call Peter's parents by their first names. They readily agreed to this request. Being courteous she asked if she could help in the kitchen. Cindy insisted she had it under control and told her she was a guest who needed to sit down and relax.

Beca ventured into the living area and noticing pictures, she asked about them. Peter pointed to one explaining, "This is my older sister, Sara, with her family. The other is my younger sister,

Amy, who is a lot like you—an independent single, living on her own."

Beca was able to look Peter in the eye because they were the same height and joshing she reprimanded him, "You never told me you had sisters!"

Around the dinner table she was informed of Peter's younger days and family history, they also asked for a rundown of her life, including how she met Peter and what her future plans were. She was willing to share her past and present, telling them of her family, her job, and how she liked biking. She also told them she was going to be an aunt again in two or three weeks, but she left them hanging when it came to what her future might be.

The afternoon slipped past quickly, and soon Peter, Ruth, and Beca were headed back toward their homes. Part way back Ruth spoke up, asking if they were going to eat soon cause she was hungry. Shortly thereafter they stopped at a fast food restaurant to satisfy Ruth and give them a short break from riding. At the restaurant Peter leaned over the table to be closer to Beca while Ruth was content eating her fries. In a gentle whisper he said to her, "My parents told me not to let you go. You must have made a good first impression." Then he asked, "So, when do I get to make a good first impression on your parents?"

Caught up in the moment, speaking before thinking it through she blurted out, "Why not tonight? My parents are always home on Sunday evenings; let's just get it over with so they can meet Ruth too."

Peter, visibly surprised, quickly replied, "Why not? Great idea, Beca! I'm sure Ruth doesn't mind; we probably would just go home and be bored anyway."

After last night and a full day already, Beca was tired, but she had backed herself into a corner and now needed to save face and follow through.

Beca rang her parents' doorbell and waited, she was nervous, wondering how her parents might react to the surprise intrusion. As Josh Stone opened the door he stated, "This is a surprise." Then he invited his daughter and her friend in. He shouted into the house warning his wife that they had company. She inquired back, "Who is it?"

Her father let the three into the house and closed the door behind them. They ventured into the living room where Elaine Stone was sitting.

Slightly embarrassed for the unannounced intrusion, Beca started with the formal introductions. Mom, Dad, this is Peter Bell and his daughter, Ruth. This is the guy I bought my car from and have been dating for about three months. I met his parents today, and he asked if he could meet mine, so here we are."

She remembered she had told them about both guys but did not have a chance to tell them what had happened last night. Now she hoped nothing embarrassing would slip into any conversations they might have.

Josh Stone introduced himself and his wife, Elaine, to Peter. Giving him a firm handshake, he commented, "This young man has a good grip, he must work with his hands."

Elaine offered something to eat or drink, but Peter informed them they had just eaten and were all set. They sat for about forty-five minutes getting to know each other best they could in the limited amount of time. Peter indicated he needed to get Ruth home to bed soon. She was tired and showed signs of boredom listening to the adults.

Back at Beca's house, Peter walked her to the door where he spoke softly. "Thank you for today. I have truly enjoyed every minute of it." Then he kissed her lightly on the lips before turning back to his car and his daughter, Ruth.

Entering the house, Beca felt drained—both emotionally and physically. Her emotions had gone from one end of the spectrum to the other in only twenty-four hours. She made sure Missy had her needs met before going directly to the bedroom. She set the alarm for work the next day because she certainly didn't want another jumpstart morning, then she crashed.

When Beca arrived home after work on Monday, the answering machine was blinking. The first message was her mother, simply stating to call her when she had a chance. Beca knew what that meant, her mother wanted to talk about her weekend. The second message was from Jason. He also just asked her to call him when she had a chance. Her mother could wait, but what did Jason want? Wasn't it over? She knew it was going to bug her to no end unless she called to discuss whatever he had on his mind. She just couldn't ignore it, but presently her emotions were still too fragile.

She acted like a zombie as she prepared her dinner. Her mind venturing deep into thought. She scolded herself for having created a situation that eventually had to hurt someone, and now she had to live with the ripple effects. The dinner gone and dishes cleaned up, Beca felt obligated to return Jason's phone call. Lifting the receiver, she hesitated then placed it back in the cradle. "Why and how did it ever come to this?" she asked herself out loud. Pushing for the relief that could only come with a completed task, she picked the receiver back up and dialed the number.

"Hello," Jason answered with no particular emotion.

Beca remembered he had caller ID, so there was no need to introduce herself, especially if he was expecting her call. She responded by saying, "Jason, I'm returning your call." She waited nervously, having no idea why he had wanted to talk to her.

"Beca," he began; this time she could hear emotion in his voice as he talked. "I want you to know I still care about you, and if there is anyway we can work this out..." he hesitated before continuing, "I'm willing to talk."

Her mind raced as she thought, *Please don't make this any harder than it already is.* He continued as she listened. "If it doesn't work out with this other guy you're seeing, I'll still be here. I'm not willing to let you go that easy. I also promise not to hold any of this against you."

He stopped talking, expecting a response. She knew it was her turn. The words did not come easy as she slowly reacted to his plea. "Thank you for being so kind," she replied. "I am so, so sorry for the way this all happened, especially right after we had such a nice dinner together. I will keep you in mind, but please don't wait for me if someone else comes along."

With neither having more to say, they simply said good-bye. Beca felt relieved, shameful, and drained all at the same time.

Trying to escape from reality, Beca slipped into a warm bubble bath with a CD playing in the background. Soaking away the anxieties while placing her mind in neutral, she just wanted to hide from the world for a while. After the rejuvenating bath, she thought she'd better call her mother before she worried about her. So, once again that evening she picked up the receiver and made a call she really didn't want to.

The first thing out of her mother's mouth as soon as she knew it was her daughter was, "We approve, honey."

Beca stuttered trying to recover from the initial shock, saying, "You...you approve of wh...what?"

"You know," her mother replied. "Peter! We approve of Peter. Your father and I also both adore his very well behaved, darling daughter."

"How can you say you approve?" Her voice went up an octave. "You talked to him for forty-five minutes."

"First impressions tell us he's a good catch," her mother continued, then asked, "When do we get to meet the other guy you're dating?"

Momentary silence fell before Beca responded, "We sorta broke up Saturday night. Look, Mom," she quickly injected. "I really can't talk anymore tonight. I gotta go." She said a hasty good-bye and hung up, giving her mother no opportunity for a rebuttal.

TIME TOGETHER

Within an hour of each other Monday evening, both Rhonda and Jillian had called her, wondering how her weekend had gone. She knew they cared, but she was to the point of not wanting to talk anymore that evening, so she quickly highlighted to each of them how she had broken off one relationship, and the other seemed to be progressing. She determined if the phone rang again, she was letting the answering machine pick it up. Missy was the only one that was going to hear her voice until tomorrow.

Thursday evening Peter called to set up another date with her. His baritone voice was becoming more familiar with time. She asked what new activity he had up his sleeve for a date. She was noticing he liked to do something different each time, keeping things interesting and exciting while getting to know each other.

Sure enough, he had another idea for them, suggesting they go Christmas shopping. "After all, it is the first week of December," he stated. "I usually don't shop until the week before, but I'll make an exception this year." He laughed lightly.

Typical male, she thought, then she pushed the issue by asking, "Is this Saturday too soon? Next Saturday, it's possible I may need to go visit my new niece or nephew if they happen to arrive early." Beca informed Peter that this time she would drive to his house, saving him drive time because he lived close to the mall. She actually had another motive; she wanted to see inside his house.

He agreed to the terms only if she came after 3:00 p.m., and he bought her dinner that evening. He asked if she preferred the time with or without Ruth. She eagerly requested she come along, asking, "How can I get to know her if I don't see her?"

Saturday morning it was snowing, with predictions of a possible two or three inches. Beca was thrilled to see the snow, thinking it added to the ambiance of the Christmas season. She arrived at Peter's home fifteen minutes after three, explaining the roads slowed her down because they were slicker than she had expected. He transferred Ruth's car seat to Beca's car after she had volunteered to drive to the mall, indicating her car was already warm.

After wandering through the mall for a couple of hours, Peter pointed to the food court stating it was time to eat. Beca exclaimed, "This is the dinner you promised me?"

"I just said I'd buy dinner," he replied, looking mischievously at her.

She smiled at his candor and replied, "All right, let's go get some food." She leaned over to ask Ruth what kind of food she wanted to eat.

Of all the places Beca thought *why here, why now?* Peter had just asked her while eating in the middle of the food court and with Ruth sitting right here, if she had been thinking about her relationship with God. She was annoyed by his thoughtlessness, so looking around she asked, "Do you think this is the appropriate time and place?"

"Absolutely," Peter exclaimed loudly, over the noise in the crowded food court. If you can't be who you really are in an awkward situation, the odds are you are only fooling yourself. I want to know the genuine Beca Stone."

Immediately she felt conviction weighing heavy. Over the past few weeks, she had thought about her lack of commitment to Christ, but had changed nothing. Peter speculated she was pondering his comment, so he waited patiently for her response.

"You're right," she finally began while she gazed into Peter eyes. I know because of the sacrifice Jesus made on the cross, that when I asked God to forgive me of my sins he did. But I've been just going through the motions ever since, never giving him first place. Now I'm ready to make the commitment of having a personal relationship, instead of a religion of rituals and right answers.

Peter replied, "If you're serious, let's pray right now, right here."

She did not hesitate, bowing her head in the crowded food court. She prayed out loud, asking God's forgiveness for her lack of commitment. When she lifted her head she said to Peter, "Thank you for being frank. For showing me that relationships are two sided. I know Christ never left me, and now I have come back to him."

Peter smiled as he commented, "Beca, I am so happy for you. This is what life is all about."

A full minute drifted by as they continued eating their lunch. Suddenly Beca blurted out, "Peter, I have another confession to make."

Peter, completely in the dark about where she was going with this blunt remark, slowly and simply questioned, "Okay?"

Beca's face turned red as she started by saying. "Now that I'm being convicted of how I live, I need be up front with you. I've been dating someone else at the same time I've been dating you, but as of a week ago it's over."

The secret was revealed. Beca felt relieved it was in the open but was very concerned what reaction may occur. She could hardly believe she had confessed, especially on the spur of the moment. Now she watched his face for any initial indication of response. Ruth unexpectedly butted in by asking, "Don't you like my daddy?" She almost broke down hearing Ruth's plea, still waiting for Peter to say something, anything.

Peter folded his hands. He first looked at Ruth then over at Beca, meeting her searching eyes. The food court was full of people, but the table of three was completely disconnected with the surroundings, time stood still. "I had no idea," Peter began, still expressionless. "Is there anything else I should know?"

She pathetically replied, "No, now you know it all." She hung her head in humiliation.

"Honesty is always the best policy," Peter began. He reached over the table to hold her hand. He continued, "I love you, Beca Stone. I forgive you for things in the past, just as Christ has forgiven us. You now have a clean slate." As she lifted her head she was warmed by his smile. "So don't you think you should answer Ruth?"

She turned toward Ruth, tightening her grip on Peter's hand while looking at her and answered, "Of course I like your daddy, and I like you too."

"Enough shopping for today," Peter said to Ruth. "Maybe Beca will take us home now."

When they arrived at the house, Peter invited her in as she had hoped. Once inside the house she was impressed as Peter showed her around his humble dwelling, pointing out several items of furniture he had made in his workshop. He explained his workshop was on the backside of the garage, but he had not had time recently, explaining Ruth was his biggest responsibility. Then he added with cheerfulness in his voice, "I've also been spending time with a special young lady."

They sat down to talk for a few minutes, with Ruth quietly playing in her bedroom. Peter calmly asked, "So do I know the other guy?"

Beca thought briefly, contemplating whether she even needed to discuss the issue but remembered they might attend the same church. "Maybe," she replied. "His name is Jason Crane. You may know him from church; he's the guy that totaled my car."

"Yes," Peter answered. "I do know who he is, but that's about all. I guess I should thank him for totaling your car, otherwise I probably would not have met you. I'm pleasantly surprised there is not more competition for such a beautiful, confident, independent, multitalented, ambitious young woman like you." She simply smiled, soaking in the compliments, wanting to freeze the moment in time.

The snow had stopped falling, leaving everything outside covered in a crisp white blanket. Together they sat in the living room, looking out the bay window, enjoying the peacefulness. They felt comfortable together without having to speak.

"Do you want something to drink or to munch on?" he asked her.

So relaxed, Beca was startled by his sudden question. She answered, "No, but I would like to see the workshop you told me you had behind the garage."

Peter checked on his daughter before they made their way to the workshop for a few minutes. Beca told him she was impressed with how organized and clean he kept it.

He reminded her he had not been able to do much in the shop over the past few months due to other responsibilities. Then added sarcastically, "It doesn't get dirty if it isn't used."

Back in the house, Beca mentioned she should probably head home. The date seemed to be winding down, and because she had driven to his house, she felt awkward to be the one deciding how and when their time together ended.

Peter put her at ease, replying, "Ruth and I do need to go grocery shopping sometime today. Maybe this sounds weird, but do you want to assist us?"

She knew without any explanation he was giving her an opportunity to choose more time together, or make an exit without feeling guilty.

Grateful for the consideration, she replied, "It is early, and I do need a few things myself." So she readily agreed to assist them, not really wanting the time to end when it was going so well. She even suggested they take one car saying, "If I'm going to assist I expect to do the whole job, which includes putting them in their place when we return." Peter was not going to argue; he had hoped she wanted to stay.

"We are taking my car, because I already have the car seat back in there, and we need to share drive time," Peter insisted.

She conceded to his demand, stating with a twinkle in her eye, "I was hoping you wouldn't use all my gas up."

Beca didn't know where to find things because the grocery store was new to her. However the experience was an eye-opening highlight with Ruth helping. Apparently she had been there numerous times before and knew where most things were located. Peter commented she was his big helper, he too had spent time hunting for items when he started shopping on his own. "Now," he stated, "Ruth and I look forward to shopping together as father and daughter."

Back at the house with groceries put away, Peter told Beca it was now so close to dinnertime that she may as well stay. Appealing to her taste buds before she responded, he added, "I was thinking maybe hot dogs or brats on the grill." Ruth—overhearing her father—butted in, shouting, "Yeah! I love hot dogs."

A smile spread across Beca's face when she heard Ruth's enthusiasm, so she answered, "That's the best offer I've had so far; I better not turn it down."

The two adults shared the responsibilities of cleaning up after the meal. Directly afterward, Beca told Peter she really did need to go home. He escorted her to the door out of Ruth's sight. There they embraced in a hug before kissing and saying "good-bye."

Thursday evening after work, Beca had a message on the answering machine from Jake and Kris. The baby had come a few days early as expected. "Another boy!" exclaimed Kris. "We named him Kevin Daniel."

Everything had gone well and Kris was expected to be home sometime Saturday. Beca preferred to visit them at their home, so she called Kris at the hospital to congratulate her and Jake before confirming a good time to visit them Saturday.

On Saturday Beca was able to get all her necessary chores done at home, before heading to Jakes home in the early afternoon. The roads were dry, and she was in good spirits as she cranked up the CD player in the car.

She was excited to see her new nephew, while spending a couple of hours with the rest of the family. Looking in awe at the baby, she asked to hold him. Kris gently handed him to her, asking, "Who do you think he looks like?"

She responded sharply, "He looks like Kevin. You are your own little man, aren't you?" she asked the baby while memorizing his face and checking out his delicate features.

While the two girls were spending a couple of minutes alone with the baby, Kris boldly asked her how things were progressing in her personal life. Before she had a chance to answer, Kris informed her that Mom and Dad were at the hospital yesterday, "They kinda filled us in on some new developments." Kris continued, "Don't be upset with your parents; they care, and so do we."

Beca butted in, "Will you stop talking? How can I fill you in if you don't give me a chance?" She handed Kevin back to Kris before stating. "I guess if Mom and Dad filled you in there is not much more to tell. Yes, I am down to one man now, and I believe it is going as well as can be expected. I spent almost a full day with Peter and his daughter, Ruth, last week." She filled Kris in on most of the activities that had taken place, including how she made a commitment to God in the middle of the food court.

Kris smiled acknowledging approval but made no comment.

It was Sunday afternoon before Beca received a call from Peter. They talked briefly before Peter asked when she was available for time together. She put Peter on the spot shyly informing him, it was her thirty-third birthday this coming Friday. "Maybe someone will take me someplace special to celebrate," she hinted.

Peter exclaimed, "I had no idea it was your birthday. You certainly know how to keep a secret." He excitedly proclaimed, "Sign me up. I will get a sitter for Ruth so it's just the two of us, how does six sound?"

"I will need to get back to you," she joshed. "I want to see what other offers come in before I make a decision."

"All right," Peter returned her off-the-wall humor. "I'll buy and also promise not to drool during dinner."

She laughed and confirmed she would be ready at six o'clock Friday evening. Then she firmly added, "I expect something better than the mall food court. I'm dressing up for this one."

Friday came quickly with Christmas only a week away, and Beca had been busy. Final decorations, shopping, food and goody preparations, it all gave the spirit of Christmas proper atmosphere. Sometimes she felt slighted for having a birthday so close to the holiday, but this year was different. The doorbell brought her back to the present. When she opened the door, Peter started singing "Happy Birthday." He stood there holding a single red rose, melting her heart.

"Enough already," she blurted. "It's too cold to just stand here."

She took the rose and placed it inside before grabbing her jacket, locking the door, and heading for his car just a few feet away. Peter opened the door for her, commenting how he had the car nice and warm just for her.

"Where are we going?" she asked once they started down the road.

"It wouldn't be a surprise if I told you up front. I assure you it's someplace better than the mall food court," he said with a gleam in his eye that forced her to smile.

She figured it out before they arrived but didn't let on she was familiar with the area.

"Here we are," Peter proudly exclaimed, pulling into the parking lot of The Barn restaurant. He stated, "I tried hard to find something unique or different. I thought this looked interesting. "Have you ever eaten here before?"

She answered in a no big deal fashion, "Yes, a couple of times. It's really nice; you made a good choice."

Dinner went well, they talked about how Peter had introduced himself at the door when he picked her up; they both laughed. She told him she was glad nobody else saw it, because he was embarrassing. I still need to go Christmas shopping for a few people he mentioned. Beca asked him if he knew he had less than a week and that some family celebrations had already taken place.

"Well," he replied, "it's actually just Ruth and maybe you I need to get something for."

Drawn in by his hint of a gift, she asked, "So what kind of gift should I expect?"

Peter leaned on the table, getting closer to Beca, so she also leaned forward in anticipation. He looked into her eyes momentarily before simply saying, "Oh, I don't know, maybe a stuffed animal or a new snow shovel." He sat back and shoved a forkful of potatoes into his mouth with a smirk on his face.

"You tease," she scolded, sighing heavily before she also resumed eating.

Winding down the meal, Peter bluntly asked her if she had any intention of him spending time with her family at Christmas. She silently thought to herself, *he sure waited until the last minute to ask something so important*, but she did not answer in any demeaning manner. She replied, "If you are able to, my family meets at my parents' home on Christmas day. We get there about ten and have brunch together."

"Is Ruth invited?" he asked, not wanting to assume anything.

"Of course," she answered, "and before you ask, I already told my mom you and Ruth may be coming."

"You're a good woman," he shot back at her, "always one step ahead of me. We accept the offer. Do you want me to pick you up or meet you there?"

"If you don't pick me up, I will be offended," she retaliated. "Besides, how would that look to my family? You showing up ten minutes before me, or something to that affect. It'd look like we aren't even together!"

Peter saw the error he made and quickly apologized, asking her what time she wanted to be picked up.

It was still early when they arrived back at Beca's home. She had anticipated doing something else after the meal, but Peter had driven directly back to her house. Disappointed, she felt an obligation to invite him in because it was still early. He turned her down, stating he was not able to secure a sitter for Ruth for very long this evening and needed to pick her up before it got too late.

Peter walked her to the door, where she gave him a quick peck on the cheek, letting him know in a subtle way she was not happy. He had not informed her ahead of time that the night was going to end so soon. Once inside the house, she suddenly thought, *It's my birthday and Peter never gave me a gift*. She felt betrayed.

Making a cup of hot chocolate to drown her sorrows, she continued to tell herself, maybe this wasn't the right man for her; he was so inconsiderate. He never even mentioned getting her something for her birthday, only Christmas, and he joked about that. The more she thought about what took place that evening the more worked up she got.

MIND GAMES

When the phone rang, Beca answered with a gruff "Hello," matching the mood she was in. The date with Peter had ended on a sour note as far as she was concerned, simply because he had forgotten about her birthday. It was Peter saying he was sorry for the way the evening had ended. "I wanted it to be a special surprise, but I'm not sure it worked out that way." He didn't give her a chance to reply, telling her he had left something special for her birthday just outside her door.

She heard the dial tone as he abruptly hung up, her mood still in the dumper she muttered, "Happy birthday, Beca."

Curious, she opened the door and peered outside. She found a long cardboard box next to the house and took it inside. Opening it up, she found he had made her custom miniature garden tools all out of oak wood; the set included a shovel, rake, and a hoe.

She wondered why he hadn't given them to her personally; maybe he forgot until after they said good-bye and didn't know how else to handle it under the circumstances. Either way, she now felt ashamed and called him to set things right. Peter accepted part of the responsibility for his actions, admitting he actually did forget about the gift in his trunk until after she had gone into the house.

Christmas morning, Peter, Beca, and Ruth were seated around the crowded table at the Stone family home for brunch. The boys were slightly skeptical of a girl invading their territory, but Ruth soon won them over with her boldness and talkative manner. Both Peter and Beca were happy to see her fit in with the family, even if she did get extra attention being the only girl.

Halfway through the gift opening, a small box was handed to Beca. Everybody speculated, making suggestions as to what it might be. Beca held her breath knowing Peter had surprised her a few times before and knew well enough not to jump to conclusions. Peter sat next to her with a suspicious smile while she slowly opened the box.

Inside the box were a note and a picture. The picture was of an oak end table with a small drawer underneath. The note read, "This is a picture of your Christmas present from Ruth and I. We did not want to bring it today, so we just brought a picture instead. We will deliver it to your home some other time."

The reaction from the family was subdued as each admired the photo.

Returning to her home later in the day, Beca turned to Peter and confessed. "You really had my heart pumping today with that small box routine, or was that your intention?" she asked.

He quickly inquired back, "What were you expecting?"

She replied just as quickly, "I have come to expect that everything from you has the purpose of keeping life interesting."

He just smiled as he reached over to hold her hand, nothing more needed to be said.

Beca spent New Year's Day with Peter's family, finally meeting his two sisters, Sara and Amy, for the first time.

It was as if they had been friends for years, talking about everything and anything. Peter interrupted them a few times, indicating he thought Beca was with him. He also brashly told his sisters, he had no intention of letting her spend enough time with them to become like them. All three girls laughed at him, while Sara, his older sister, told him he should be so lucky.

Over the next month, Peter and Beca talked or met at least every other day. She knew Valentine's Day was coming soon. She traced back the memory of the past five months they had been dating. All her friends told her it was time for Peter to make a move, because from their perspective they were already a couple. She tried to imagine life the way it was before she had the accident last June. Since that time she had met so many new friends, and explored many different places. Her thoughts escaped as she said out loud to her empty house, "My life was missing so much, and I didn't even know it!"

Only about a week before Valentine's Day, the snow was falling again, adding to the fifteen inches already on the ground. Beca showed up at Peter's house that Saturday afternoon so the three of them could go to the mall for something to do together. They watched people while sitting on one of the benches in the mall until Ruth could sit no more. They wandered through a few stores then stopped for ice cream before heading back to the house.

At the Bell home, Ruth begged her daddy to take her outside to build a snowman. Beca encouraged him to go play while she searched for something to make for dinner. He gave her a quick hug and told Ruth to get dressed so they could play in the snow.

Father and daughter played in the snow while Beca prepared a dinner of chicken strips and instant potatoes that she had found in the pantry. She watched them through the bay window from the warmth of the living room, while they attempted to make a snowman with the fluffy snow. She whispered out loud, "So this is what it feels like," referring to having a family of her own. She smiled, thinking Peter just might ask her to be his wife on Valentine's Day. Her friends were right; it was time to make a move. She didn't want to let go of something within her grasp, something she had long desired.

Beca now knew Peter was Mr. Right for her. He was gentle, kind, good looking, sincere, and committed to God in everything he did.

She called outside that dinner was ready, so they came in shivering and exhausted. They got the coats and boots off before they made their way to the bathroom to wash up for dinner. Seated at the table, Peter asked Ruth if she wanted to ask the blessing on the meal. She smiled then said "yes." She held her hands out for Beca and her father to hold, then she prayed.

While dishing up potatoes for Ruth, Beca said to her, "Look at me."

The little girl—puzzled—looked up at her and asked, "Why?"

She calmly said, "I have a question I want to ask you. Is it okay if I become your mommy?"

Peter almost dropped the plate of chicken strips he was holding. His eyes widened and his mouth opened like he was preparing to speak. Beca held her finger to her lips, indicating she desired him to be quiet.

Ruth started spreading the potatoes around on her plate as she simply answered, "I guess so."

Beca continued, "Don't you think it would be nice if I lived here all the time? Then we could do girl stuff together, we could be a family."

Peter was trying to protest, but again she held her finger up, letting him know she wanted him to wait. This time Ruth lit up and asked, "We can be a family? Me and Daddy and you? Together all the time?"

Beca turned to face Peter and asked, "Is there any reason you can give your daughter for not letting me be her mommy?"

"Now, just a minute," Peter finally was able to muster. "I may have had intentions for the future, but this is not the way, the time, or the place!"

On a roll now, Beca didn't back down. Still addressing Peter, she stated, "I believe you are usually the one with a surprise or two up his sleeve; now it's my turn." She boldly told him to answer the question, while she placed the bowl of potatoes on the table next to him.

He slowly began, "At the present time, I cannot come up with a single reason."

She abruptly cut him off by asking, "Well then, will you marry me?"

Peter was dumbfounded as it all happened so fast and unexpected. Stunned, he answered slowly, never taking his eyes off her, "Of course I will."

They got up from their chairs and embraced in a hug of confirmation. Ruth excitedly exclaimed, "I got a mommy, yeah!"

After things settled down, Peter said, "I was planning to ask you in about a month from now. Do me a favor, don't tell anybody how this happened, it's terribly embarrassing."

"You should have thought of that sooner," she scolded. "You knew you were dating a confident, independent, ambitious woman, and I'm not getting any younger!

Ruth interrupted them by asking if she could have some chicken. Peter compassionately answered "yes," then suggested they all just settle down and enjoy the meal.

Beca commented, "I will have an instant family; we will go bike riding, camping, hiking; Ruth and I can do girl stuff together. There is so much to do, I have to call my family and all my friends, then she hesitated. Looking at Peter with a gleam in her eye she stated, "We need to talk about how soon Ruth will have siblings."

Peter quickly replied, "Slow down, one step at a time, one step at a time."

"There is one stipulation connected to this union," she demanded. "The car is mine."

Peter laughed, replying, "You drive a hard bargain, Beca Stone."

Cutting him off again, she asked, "So where is my ring, Mr. Bell?"

He suddenly got the deer in the headlight look before asking, "Didn't you ask me? Where is *my* ring, future Mrs. Bell?"

She knew she had been had this time. Peering into Peter's eyes she stated, "I love you, Peter Bell." He sat motionless for a few seconds as if trying to figure something out then said, "this is wrong!"

Alarmed she asked, "What's wrong?"

He got up from his chair and stood beside her. I'm a traditionalist, so I want to do this right."

Beca's breathing was shallow as Peter got down on one knee and held both her hands. "Beca Stone, will you marry me?"

She tenderly answered, "Yes, Peter. I will marry you."

Neither one moved but seemed frozen in the moment. Both again were breathing normal, smiles spreading slowly across their faces.

Ruth was eating, oblivious to what was taking place just across the table. Finally Peter returned to his chair saying, "I really don't have a ring for you yet."

She quickly answered, "Good."

Peter, taken back slightly, asked, "What do you mean, good?

"Well," she replied, "We can go shopping for matching rings, and I can pick out a nice big one for myself. This is going to be the best Valentine's Day ever!"

Peter reminded her she was eating chicken strips and instant potatoes, indicating what economic class she was entering into. "Beca," he said, while looking tenderly into her eyes. "I could never have imagined Linda's car or you having an accident bringing us together. I am so happy and look forward to the years of memories we will make together as a family."

Beca simply smiled. There was nothing more to be said.